MW01267948

The Frozen Prince

Minna Louche

DDP
DEEP DESIRES PRESS
Winnipeg, Canada

Copyright © 2019 by Minna Louche
Cover design copyright © 2019 by Story Perfect Dreamscape

All characters are age 18 and over.

This is a work of fiction. Names, characters, business, places, events, and incidents are either products of the author's imagination or used in a fictitious manner. Any resemblances to actual persons, living or dead, or actual events is purely coincidental.

No part of this book may be used or reproduced in any manner without written permission from the publisher. However, brief quotations may be reproduced in the context of reviews.

Published June 2019 by Deep Desires Press, an imprint of Story Perfect Inc.

Deep Desires Press
PO Box 51053 Tyndall Park
Winnipeg, Manitoba R2X 3B0
Canada

Visit http://www.deepdesirespress.com for more scorching hot erotica and erotic romance.

WIN FREE BOOKS!
Subscribe to our email newsletter to get notified of all our hot new releases, sales, and giveaways! Visit deepdesirespress.com/newsletter to sign up today!

The Frozen Prince

Chapter One

"THIS WAY!" GENEVIEVE CRIED OUT AS she and Malaya ran down the hall at full speed, pursued by their tutor. Malaya might have been a princess, and Genevieve only a wash girl, but the two seven-year-olds were inseparable friends and partners in crime. With Malaya's status, and Genevieve's growing knowledge of the castle's hidden secrets, the two were unstoppable.

"In here!" Genevieve pushed a painting aside, revealing a hole in the bricks of the great hall—a hidden passage.

"When did you find this one?" Malaya asked excitedly, crawling inside.

"Just yesterday." Genevieve pushed the painting back into place behind her, just as the tutor came running by. She could hear him shouting, and the two girls giggled.

Their friendship wasn't exactly a secret—Genevieve was the only other child Malaya's age living in the castle, so their bond had been unavoidable, but the mix of classes was frowned upon. As a result, the two girls often hid themselves away, especially during lesson time.

"Come on, this leads up over the ballroom."

They climbed the narrow staircase until they reached the ceiling. There was a hole where the chandelier hung, and they could look down easily without being seen.

"It's great because I can spy on parties," Genevieve grinned. The girl was a skinny mess of freckles and brown hair. Scrapes covered her knees and her nose was smudged with dirt.

"I wish you could come to the parties," Malaya said. She had a plump figure and lighter and tamer hair than her friend.

There was no denying their class differences, but when they were like this—both dresses covered in dust and cobwebs, faces flushed with happiness—they felt no difference.

"Well, whenever you're down there, dancing and meeting fancy people, you can glance up at the ceiling and give me a little wave."

Their spying was interrupted by an urgent voice. They looked down to see a squire running across the ballroom. "Your majesty!" he called.

"It's dad!" Malaya giggled, pointing out the king.

"Sire," the squire sounded frightened, "there's a disturbance in the north!"

They watched as the king and squire both hurried out of the room.

"What's going on?" Genevieve wondered.

"My balcony faces north, let's go look."

They both stood and hurried off, eager to be part of the action.

Outside, it was a beautiful summer day, a breeze swept over them as the girls stepped out onto the balcony from Malaya's bedroom. Down below they could see that the king and several knights had lined up, fully armored.

In the distance, they could clearly see the snow-capped mountains of the north. They provided a beautiful view, but at that moment, they looked ominous and bleak as a large storm cloud formed over them. The girls could hear the distant rumble of thunder.

"What's wrong?" Genevieve asked. "It's just a storm."

"Dad's afraid of the Northern Mountain," Malaya said, "he talks about it a lot with his advisors, and sometimes he looks at it through his telescope."

"Why? What's out there?"

Malaya shrugged.

There was a shout from below, and the knights mounted their horses, riding off towards the storm. The king watched them go, then returned to the castle.

Genevieve watched as well, curiosity growing, but her thoughts were interrupted by a knock at the door.

"Malaya, are you in there?" the tutor's voice demanded.

Genevieve didn't waste any time. She ran to Malaya's wardrobe and slipped inside. Behind the rows of clothes there was yet another passage, which led outside to the stables. This was Genevieve's favorite secret, because it allowed her to not only sneak into Malaya's room for playtime, but to secretly attend lessons. Genevieve would sit comfortably amongst the coats and dresses, listening and following along. She even kept a slate and chalk in the passage.

Genevieve was used to secrecy. As a baby her mother, a laundry woman, had kept her hidden until she was five and old enough to work. Shadowy corners, nooks and crannies, and hidden passages were in her blood, and Genevieve never felt more comfortable and in control than when she was safely hidden, able to spy and sneak.

The tutor entered the room and scolded Malaya as she sat down to resume the class.

"If you run off again, I will inform your father and have you locked—"

"Sir," Malaya interrupted, "could I ask you a history question?"

Genevieve peeked through the cracked wardrobe door. The tutor gave Malaya an exasperated look.

"No, really!" Malaya said, "I want to know about the Northern Mountain. Why did father send knights there just now?"

Genevieve put her ear to the crack, eager to know as well.

"It's more hearsay than history, but your father takes it seriously, so I suppose an overview wouldn't hurt," the tutor said, "there was a kingdom in the north, until it was overthrown by a revolution. The royal family was killed, but there is a rumor that the prince survived in...an unexpected way..."

The young prince ran, heart hammering, sweat rolling in

the heat of the flames. The castle was burning, and his mother's screams still echoed in his ears.

Run.

Run.

The peasants from the nearby village were attacking, revolting. They attacked the castle while everyone slept and started the fire. His mother had pulled him from his bed, urging him to get out and hide. He didn't even have time for shoes.

He snuck through the servants' halls, trying to find an exit. In the kitchen, he finally found a door leading outside, but shouting stopped him from continuing his run. Gasping for air, the prince looked through the crack of the door.

He saw his parents, the king and queen, kneeling in the snow, surrounded by rebels. To the young prince, they looked like monsters, skinny from starvation, covered in animal fur to protect them from the hard winter that had plagued their mountain-top kingdom for months.

His parents told him food was in short supply from the long winter, and there was disease spreading through the villages. They said the villagers were becoming restless and angry. He never understood how angry they truly were.

The people were screaming at his parents, accusing them of hiding food, living in luxury while they starved. He saw a broad man march through the snow towards them, carrying an ax. He reached the king and queen and raised the weapon over his head.

A hand came down on the prince's face and pulled

him away from the door. The prince cried out in fear, but looking up, saw his royal knight standing over him, looking haggard and holding a bloody sword.

"Mom and dad—"

"Shh," the knight warned, "I'm sorry my prince...I'm sorry. I have to get you out of here."

He took the prince's arm and led him back through the castle, toward the rear gates. Outside a storm was raging, the blizzard filled the air with snow, making it difficult to breathe.

There was a shout. Somehow, the villagers had spotted them.

The prince desperately looked to his guard. The knight squeezed his shoulder, and the boy felt the fear in his grip.

"Run my prince, run." The knight stepped forward and raised his sword like a throwing knife. He was the strongest knight they had, and a force to fear against challengers, but tonight, against the mob, he seemed as helpless as the prince felt. He heaved his sword with a mighty throw. It cartwheeled through the air. The blade impaled the chest of an oncoming villager.

"Run!" The knight ordered. He charged forward to meet the mob. The prince went the opposite way, running for the trees where he might be able to hide.

His hands and feet were numb. The wind was on his skin like the lashing of a whip. His tears were turning to ice on his cheeks. The prince realized that even if he was able to hide, he wouldn't survive this night.

When he reached the tree line, a figure stepped out of

the shadows, its features hidden by the burning fire behind them. To the prince, it just seemed another monster.

He felt a sharp pain in his chest as the figure struck him. The prince placed his hands over the pain, and brought them back, finding blood. He stumbled away, and the figure left him.

The prince wandered into the trees, walking deep into the forest until his legs collapsed beneath him. He hit the ground, and immediately felt the snow begin to build up over him, burying him.

Then it felt as if something was there with him. Some creature inspecting him. Perhaps it was a wolf looking for a meal, or death coming to lead him away. The prince closed his eyes, not caring.

Do you wish to live? a voice asked.

"Yes."

To take revenge?

"Yes."

The ice seemed to be inside him, crawling in through his wound, into his blood, stopping it from flowing out of his body.

How badly do you want this?

"With all my heart."

Then, his heart stopped beating.

"I'm not sure whether the next part is true," the tutor said, "but survivors have sworn it. They say that the prince rose from the snow like a body out of a grave. He came out of the woods, skin like ice, his eyes like frost. They said his wound was open, but no blood flowed from it.

"He approached the rebels, and they say that ice flowed from his hands, that the storm raged where he ordered it. He put out the fire and killed those who weren't able to run away. When they came back the next day, they said they found the frozen bodies of the rebels scattered throughout the mountain. The castle still stood, but every door and window was frozen shut, barricaded in ice.

"The winter continued, lasting through the spring, and even into summer. The villagers abandoned their homes, leaving the mountain. They say it is never without snow, and when a storm arrives, it means that the prince has become angry again. Anyone who tries to approach the castle is attacked, or meets their end on the frozen tundra."

Malaya's mouth had fallen open. Genevieve gripped her chalk.

"People say the Frozen Prince is still there, cursed, forced to live in a frozen hell."

The chalk snapped in Genevieve's tightening grip. The tutor glanced toward the wardrobe. Malaya quickly brought his attention back to the story.

"Is it true? Is that why father is so vigilant?"

"I don't know if the Frozen Prince is real, but there have been other strange stories since the incident. There are caravans that go to the castle, but the drivers have no idea who the supplies are for. They said that a toymaker in a nearby town disappeared from his shop, and they found it filled with melting snow. And then, not long after, a witch had been broken out of jail, they found the bars of her cell frozen and shattered into ice."

"Did the Frozen Prince take them?"

"That's what the stories say. Your father keeps a wary eye on the mountain now, that's why he sent knights to investigate the storm. I'm not one to indulge in fantasy, but, well…"

The tutor walked across the room and opened the curtains. They could see the mountain from the window. The beautiful summer day was now covered with cloud, and from those clouds, snow was falling, a thick layer covering the summer foliage.

When the lesson was over, the girls took advantage of the strange weather to play outside. After a vigorous snowball fight, they both collapsed and made snow angels, staring up at the sky.

"Do you think the story about the Frozen Prince is true?" Genevieve asked.

"I hope not, it's so scary."

"What do you think cursed him?"

"What do you mean?"

"The tutor said that the prince had been cursed, well, curses are put on someone by something else, like an evil witch. So, who cursed the prince?"

Malaya shuddered, "I don't want to think about it. It's such a sad story, I don't know what I would do if something happened to my mom and dad."

"Yeah."

"You okay, Gen?"

"Yeah."

"I have to go inside now."

"Can't you play a little longer?"

"Sorry, I have to be on time for dinner. See you tomorrow." Malaya left, but Genevieve remained, staring at the sky until tears filled her eyes.

When she finally went inside she retreated to the laundry, where the day's laundry waited. She stirred huge barrels of boiling water full of linen, then pulled the clothes out and ran them through a laundry press, using all her strength to turn the mechanism. Finally, she hung everything up to dry. When she was done, her hair was frizzled from the humidity, her back hurt from having to stand on a stool to hang the laundry, and her hands were red and wrinkled. She opened a small window and stuck her face out, thankful for the cold air. She wiped her tears and finally called it a night.

In the servants' quarters, Genevieve brought her mother a cup of water. Usually they shared the bed, but Hanna had fallen sick, so Genevieve slept in the laundry, or fell asleep on the floor, holding her mother's hand.

"Hi, mom. Do you feel better?"

"So much better, I'll be up in no time," Hanna said, smothering a cough. She drank the water and forced a smile.

"I did all the laundry."

"You did? Oh, my sweet girl, thank you. I'm sorry you have to do so much work, but I can't let anyone know I'm sick. Might get in trouble."

Genevieve crawled into bed and rested her head on Hanna's lap. Hanna stroked her hair.

"Honey, I think that...it's time you met your father."

"I'm fine, mom. I can take care of myself. And you."

"I know you're strong, but I might not always be around, and if that happens I want you to find him."

A tear escaped Genevieve's eye, and she held onto Hanna tightly.

"I love you."

"I love you too."

A few days later, Genevieve stood at her mother's grave. A few of the servants had attended the funeral but were now gone. One tried to get her to come inside and eat, but Genevieve ignored them.

Genevieve stood there alone until the sun was completely gone.

"Gen, your father loved me very much," echoes of their last conversation played in Genevieve's head. She finally turned away from the grave and headed back to the castle. *"But we were unwed, and I was young and scared. I want you to find him. He will help you."*

A party was taking place that night. Genevieve entered the secret passage that led to the ceiling above the ballroom, and laid down flat to look through the chandelier hole to view the festivities. Around the glow of the chandelier she could see lords and ladies dancing, twirling below her. At the other end of the room tables were arranged in a horseshoe where people ate mountains of food.

In the middle of that horseshoe was the jester.

He juggled flaming torches while the men roared and laughed. One threw a goblet of wine at him, and the alcohol caught fire, burning his face and sleeve, but the Jester never dropped a torch. He threw them in the air, backflipped, and caught each one, blowing them out as they landed in his palm. Everyone cheered.

Genevieve waited until the party finally ended. In the wee hours of morning, before the last drunken lord stumbled off to bed, only then did she leave the secret passage and make her way down.

She found the Jester sitting cross-legged on a table, eating an apple. He removed his hat with a jingle of bells, and held a wet cloth to his singed face. Genevieve approached quietly, walking up behind him.

"They don't take kindly to beggars you know," the Jester said, not turning. Genevieve stopped. "Course, you might not be a beggar at all, might just be this silly fool, talking to himself. You're probably just my imagination, and I know my imagination doesn't eat sweet rolls, like that one over there."

Genevieve noted the pastry sitting nearby.

"But what do I know?" The Jester shrugged and finished his apple.

"I'm not a beggar. I work here."

The Jester finally turned around, looking at her for the first time.

"Oh?"

"My mom wanted me to find you."

"...and who is your mom?"

"Hanna."

The Jester stared at her in some shock for a moment. He turned and stood up, approaching her.

"How old are you?"

"Seven."

The jester stopped in front of her, staring in disbelief.

"My mom told me to find you if..." Genevieve stammered, "she said you were my..." she choked, unable to hold the tears back. The Jester went to his knees and hugged her tightly. Genevieve returned the hug with vigor, sobbing into his shoulder.

"It-it's okay," he said uncertainly, "I'm here. I'm here..."

Once Genevieve calmed down, the Jester took her outside, bringing the sweet roll with them. He showed her a plank bridge over the moat that the servants had built to sneak out at night. They sat on the bridge and ate the sweet roll together.

"You mother used to sneak out at night to see me. I loved her very much. I didn't understand why she broke it off between us, but now I see she was trying to hide you."

Genevieve chewed the sweet roll, not answering.

"I'm sorry for your loss, Genevieve. If I had known—"

"Will you teach me?" Genevieve cut him off.

"Teach you what?"

"The trick with the torches and the dancing."

"You want to learn to juggle?"

Genevieve nodded. She tore off three bits of pastry and tried to juggle them as she had seen the Jester do, but they easily fell into the water.

"It's pretty tricky. Start with something simple first." The Jester reached into his knapsack and pulled out two red balls. "Practice with just two first, and then I'll show you how to do three."

Genevieve smiled. The Jester smiled back.

They made a routine of meeting each other whenever they could. Genevieve was busy during the day, washing and sneaking lessons during Malaya's tutoring, but despite being exhausted, she would meet the Jester at night and they would juggle, do cartwheels, summersaults, anything that the Jester could teach. Sometimes they would make a campfire and the Jester would play his lute while Genevieve danced.

When Malaya started taking dance lessons she would teach the steps to Genevieve and they would practice together in the grass. Sometimes Genevieve danced in the laundry, twirling a broom as her partner. She longed to be part of the balls and have a real dance someday.

The Jester was pleased to hear about her lessons, and urged her to continue as she got older, insisting that she would be able to use her education to become a handmaiden or lady in waiting.

"I don't want you to be stuck here washing clothes like your mom," he insisted, "if I had known about you, I would have taken you both away from this place. As your father it's my job to make sure you get a proper life, and a good husband."

Genevieve didn't mind either way. She had grown strong from laundry work and acrobatics, and she surpassed Malaya in lessons. Her hair was thick and long, and her freckles accentuated her brown eyes. She wasn't sure what kind of life she could have, but for the time she was happy to have her father and her friends.

After they celebrated their eighteenth birthdays, Malaya was told it was time to find a suitor.

"Oh, Gen! It's terrible! I can't take this!" Malaya threw herself on her bed dramatically. Genevieve laughed. She had snuck up the secret passage from the stables so that they could gossip and visit before the daily chores began.

"Stay calm, little drama queen-to-be."

"I'm scared, Gen. The suitors are coming today. What if they're all terrible? What if I don't like any of them?"

Malaya had become a beautiful woman as well, still plump and curvy, with her hair shining, and her eyes bright. But she wasn't as confident as Genevieve.

"I can't feel sorry for you on this one, Malaya. You get to have your choice from a line of princes."

"You just don't understand. It's so stressful. I don't know any of them. What if the one I pick is charming and loving at first then turns out to be a horrible person?"

"Your father wouldn't let that happen. Besides, if any of them mistreat you, we know how to take care of him." Genevieve reached under the bed and pulled out two wooden sparring swords that Malaya kept hidden there. While Genevieve had snuck lessons from Malaya, Malaya had snuck some tutoring of her own. The two had coerced the squires into teaching them how to swordfight and practiced in the stables late at night. Genevieve tossed one of the training swords to the princess and tried to strike her. Malaya blocked it and chuckled.

"See? No one would dare lay a finger on the Mighty Malaya."

Malaya smiled gratefully. Genevieve set the swords aside, and the two shared a hug.

"Promise you'll be there, Gen? I'll feel better if I know you're watching over me."

"Of course. I want to see all the handsome princes as well!"

Someone knocked at the door, ending their visit. Genevieve quickly disappeared into the wardrobe as the door opened and Malaya's ladies in waiting entered.

"It's time to get ready, your grace."

"Very well, let's adjourn to the dressing room." Malaya said, covering the nervousness in her voice. Genevieve watched her sadly, despite her casual attitude she did worry for her friend. She retreated down the tunnel, which took her to the stables.

Genevieve returned to her chores, but was distracted by thoughts of her friend's predicament. Malaya had already promised to bring Genevieve with her when she left with her new husband, but what if she was right? What if the new castle was horrible? Genevieve couldn't just leave her father.

Then there was all the talk of husbands and suitors. Genevieve's stomach turned nervously at the thought. Perhaps her father was right, instead of following Malaya, should she be looking into her own marriage?

She pictured handsome men and started to twirl around with her broom. Perhaps she could meet a strong carpenter, muscular and protective. He wouldn't know how to dance, but she could teach him, and they could dance for their wedding.

Genevieve folded herself backward, pretending the broom was dipping her. Something in her loins stirred and she collapsed into a pile of laundry.

She would find a gentle husband…but not *too* gentle. She imagined herself on her wedding night as she guided her hand up under her skirt where she began to message herself through her undergarment. She would have to teach her husband that too. How to tease her, get her warmed up.

This was something she and Malaya had been talking about as well (with news of suitors, Malaya needed someone to teach her what to expect) and Genevieve found herself frequently enjoying private moments of self-pleasure.

She wiggled her fingers against her clitoris until she became wet and wanting. She pulled her underwear down and used the natural lubricant to slip her fingers into herself, seeking the spot that would fill her body with pleasure. Her other hand went to work on her pearl, and the combined sensations made her sigh with happiness.

Her fingers finally found the sweet place deep inside of her and she worked it vigorously, fingers pushing as far inside as she could reach. A sweet sensation began to bubble up inside of her and she began to pant with effort. She felt like a kettle starting to boil, building up, so close she felt she would explode…

Genevieve gasped as she reached her orgasm. A gorgeous feeling of release that left her body relaxed and limp. She could feel the walls of her vagina pulsing around her fingers as she came. She kept pressing on her clit until the sensitivity was too much, then removed her hands with a satisfied sigh. She laid back in the laundry and savored the euphoria as it slowly faded.

Once she had recovered, Genevieve gave up on chores and decided to seek out the Jester. She found him on the rooftop, chatting with some of the archers who were awaiting the suitors' arrival.

"Will you be performing when Malaya meets the suitors?" Genevieve asked, peering down over the castle wall to the road below.

"I'll be present, but I don't think it'll be appropriate if I perform."

"You should. Just poke fun at the suitors a bit, Malaya would appreciate it."

"I'm more interested in *your* suitors."

Genevieve frowned. "I don't have any."

"Exactly. I want you to start looking for a husband, a good man who can take care of you and get you out of that laundry."

"I don't need a husband. Malaya is going to take me with her."

The Jester beamed. "That's wonderful!"

"I'm hoping she'll take you as well."

"Aw, Gen, I don't want you to worry about me—"

Trumpeting interrupted their conversation.

"A prince is coming!" an archer announced. They all leaned forward excitedly.

"Who is that?" Genevieve asked.

"Looks like the flags of Prince Michael," the Jester said, "from the west. A prosperous kingdom."

Prince Galen, from the east, arrived next. Then Prince Kyran, from the south. The Jester knew a little bit about each.

"Kyran shares his father's love of war, they say he is quite ruthless. Galen's father is ill, and he will soon take the throne. I'm told he has a good temperament."

"Are they the only ones?" Genevieve asked skeptically. "Not much to pick from."

"I'd better get to the ballroom," the Jester said, "duty calls!"

Genevieve left the roof as well, but she wasn't about to miss out on her best friend's betrothal. She climbed up the familiar hidden staircase, and situated herself above the ballroom, where the royal family was seated on their thrones. The princes stood in a line before the royal family. Malaya was wearing a beautiful and modest gown with her hair and face obscured by a veil.

"I welcome each of you," the king said, standing. "My daughter has come of age and seeks a man of noble lineage. I have known your fathers in my youth, and I know you all to be good men. I have agreed to let my daughter have the final decision in her betrothal. She wishes to visit with each of you. Please take the day to socialize. Tonight, we will celebrate her choice with an engagement party."

Genevieve frowned. There was a strange cold creeping up through the ceiling. She could see the others shivering.

From her perspective, she could see something creeping along the floor. It looked like...

Ice.

There was a sudden bang as the doors of the main hall flew open. Genevieve almost had to hang upside down to see who had come in. A figure in a dark cloak stepped in, face hidden under a hood, snow blowing in around him, even though it was an early spring day.

The figure—who stood taller than any of the men—walked into the room. Everyone stared in confusion.

"I have come as a suitor, your majesty," the man said.

Prince Kyran drew his sword. "You were not invited here."

Genevieve watched as the man reached up and pushed the hood from his head, revealing dark hair and skin as pale as snow.

"The Frozen Prince," she gasped. Fearing for Malaya, Genevieve took a pocket knife from her dress pocket, and began to saw away at the chandelier rope.

"He has as much right to be here as the rest of us," Prince Michael said, "it is the princess's choice."

"Oh no, you misunderstand," the Frozen Prince said, walking past the others, and approaching Malaya, who stood terrified next to her parents. The prince towered over her. "She has no choice."

The king moved first, pushing Malaya behind him. Prince Kyran attacked, thrusting his sword. The Frozen Prince spun around, dodging the blow.

The door suddenly burst open again, and a group of

knights rushed in. They wore black armor, covered in frost. Guards to the Frozen Prince.

Before the knights could reach the royals, Genevieve's knife cut through the rope. The chandelier fell, crashing to the floor, and halting the knights in their attack.

Genevieve scrambled to keep her balance and pull herself back into the ceiling. As she did, she swore the Frozen Prince's eyes met hers, but only for a moment as she crawled back into the ceiling and raced to get to the secret passage.

She had to get to Malaya.

In the ballroom, the Jester grabbed the queen and Malaya, and rushed them to a side door. The king drew his sword to guard their retreat. The Frozen Prince turned on him.

The king swung his sword, but the prince grabbed his wrist easily. The king's hand turned an angry red, then white as frost crawled over his skin. The king winced and went to his knees in pain, his hand completely frozen.

The prince walked past him, after Malaya.

The queen, Jester, and Malaya ran down the hall, but the castle was in chaos as servants ran scared. Two frozen knights appeared around the corner.

"I'll distract them, you keep moving," the Jester said, pushing the queen and princess down another hall.

As the knights approached, he did a front flip and jumped in front of them.

"Oi! Isn't it cold in there?" he asked, tapping their armor.

The knights drew their swords.

"So moody! Are your peckers cold?"

The two knights push past him, chasing after the royal women.

"Wait! I'm still thinking of an ice pun!"

As the knights turned the corner, one was met with a torch to the head, wielded by the queen. The knight fell to the ground. The second knight overpowered her, taking the torch and throwing it aside. As the Jester ran up to them, the knight pointed his sword at his throat, forcing him to stop.

Malaya ran down the hall at full speed, finally reaching her bedroom. She slammed the door shut and locked it, gasping for air.

Genevieve suddenly appeared behind her, making her scream in surprise.

"It's just me!"

"Oh, Gen!" Malaya fell into her arms, sobbing.

"I know you're scared, but you have to stay calm, okay? Quickly now, take off your dress."

"Why?" Malaya gasped as Genevieve began undoing her corset.

"I'll wear it and buy you some time, make them chase me while you escape."

"No! What if they hurt you?"

A heavy pounding suddenly shook the door. The girls gasped.

"Hurry!" Genevieve helped her out of the dress and gave Malaya hers. Genevieve put on the veil to hide her hair. Malaya tried to button the back of Genevieve's gown, but her shaking hands slipped as another barrage of banging shook the door.

"Leave it! Come on."

Genevieve took Malaya to the wardrobe and pushed her in. "This leads down to the stables. Take a horse. Ride as hard as you can. Don't come back until you know it is safe."

"Come with me!"

Something struck the door again, it began to crack and splinter.

"Go!" Genevieve closed the wardrobe and spun around as the door broke open. Knights rushed in.

Genevieve ran for the French doors that led out onto the bedroom balcony. Her unbuttoned dress slipping from her shoulders. She threw the doors open and ran to the railing. The air was cold, and there was a little snow on the ground. As the knights advanced, Genevieve climbed up onto the railing.

"Stay back or I'll jump!"

The knights stopped.

Then, the Frozen Prince walked into the room.

Genevieve almost lost her balance, but she willed herself to stay calm. The prince walked out onto the balcony, staring her down. Standing on the railing, she was at eye-level with him.

"I demand that you leave this castle at once!"

"You have much authority for such a little princess," he answered, his voice as deep as a glade. He stepped up to her.

Genevieve faltered, fearful and overwhelmed. The

cold touched her shoulders and bare back, making her shiver. She stared into his eyes—white like ice. Her eyes darted down to look at his chest.

The prince noticed.

"You've heard the stories then?"

The Frozen Prince undid a button on his shirt, letting it fall open. Genevieve stared, lips parting in shock. There was an open wound on his chest, not healed, but not bleeding. He was inches from her now, frosted eyes staring into hers.

Genevieve fainted, body falling backward, threatening to fall from the balcony. The frozen prince reached one arm out casually, catching her around the waist and swinging her back around to safety.

"We are leaving now," he said, pulling Genevieve into his arms. The knights nodded and led the way out of the castle.

Down in the stables, Malaya struggled to saddle a horse. She urged the beast out of the stable with a saddle under her arm. As she attempted to saddle it again, she heard shouting from the front of the castle.

She saw with horror that the Frozen Prince was leaving—with Genevieve in his arms. The knights mounted their horses, and the prince boarded a carriage.

"No! Wait!" Malaya shouted, dropping the saddle.

A thunder of hooves filled the air as the knights and carriage took off. Malaya mounted her horse bareback and urged it to follow.

"Stop! That's not the princess!"

Without the saddle, Malaya couldn't get far. The jostling of the horse caused her to slip off and fall to the ground. She watched helplessly as the carriage disappeared into the woods.

"Genevieve!" Malaya cried.

It was then that the Jester found her sitting in the grass. Seeing the dress, he thought it was his daughter, but as he neared her…

"Your majesty? Are you alright?"

Malaya looked up at him, face streaked with tears.

"I don't understand, who did they take…?"

Then realization hit him.

Malaya started sobbing again, putting her face in her hands in remorse. The jester fell to his knees and put his arms around her. He looked after the retreating caravan, anger slowly creeping into his heart.

"Ride to the north and surround his castle! I want my daughter returned!" The king shouted, rallying his knights into formation. His hand was wrapped, and his face pained, but his voice was full of rage as he shouted orders to his men.

"Your majesty, look!" one of his knights rode to his side pointing to the side of the castle. The king turned and saw the Jester walking toward them, carrying a girl in his arms. The king recognized his daughter's shining hair and dropped his sword in relief, running toward them.

"Daddy…"

"Oh, my darling." He took Malaya from the jester and held her tightly, tears stinging his eyes.

"Daddy, they took a servant girl. She saved me. We switched dresses. Dad, please help her."

"I'm getting you to safety first."

The king led her toward the castle, putting his cape over her shoulders.

The Jester approached one of the knights. "I just saw the most powerful man in the kingdom brought to tears by a little girl."

"Such is the power of a daughter," the knight said.

"Then you'll understand."

The Jester suddenly pulled the knight off his horse. As the knight hit the ground, the Jester grabbed his sword from its sheath and pointed it threateningly.

"Stay back, Sir Knight, I have no idea how to use this thing. Someone might get hurt."

"What's this about, you fool?"

"A little girl."

The Jester grabbed the horse's reins and pulled himself up into the saddle. The other knights surrounded him.

"What's going on over there?" the king demanded, hearing the commotion.

The Jester tried to ride away, but the knights easily pulled him off the horse. The king stormed back, glaring.

"You attack one of my knights? Have you gone mad? Put him in the dungeon, I'll sort this out later."

Malaya watched, confused, as the Jester was dragged away. The king returned to her, putting a comforting arm around her shoulders.

"Father, aren't you going to go after the prince?"

"There will be an attack, but he is a...unique opponent," the king looked at his bandaged hand. "It's frostbite, I may lose the hand. I need to think carefully about this."

"But he'll kill the girl when he finds out it's not me!"

"I need time to formulate a plan. I'm sorry, Malaya, what she did for you was noble, but I cannot risk the few men I have to go after her."

"You were going to do it for me!"

"You're my daughter."

As the words sank in, Malaya turned her head back to the jester who was forcefully being dragged away. Her eyes widened in understanding.

The Jester sat in the dungeon impatiently. Time was of the essence! Try as he might, he couldn't find a way out of the cell. As he began to formulate a complicated plan to dig his way out with a spoon, the door opened.

The princess stepped in.

"Princess? What are you doing?"

He was surprised to see that Malaya was dressed in pants and boots, and carried a bag on her shoulder.

"You're Genevieve's father, aren't you?"

He gave a small nod in response.

"She never told me," Malaya shook her head, "she never told me anything. She was always looking after me."

"She valued your friendship," the Jester said.

"She is so much stronger than me. I was always so envious. I thought that she was much more of a princess than I."

"Do you want to go after her?" the Jester asked.

Malaya nodded.

"Then let's go."

They snuck through the castle together, using the secret passages to avoid the guards. The Jester went to his quarters and quickly packed a bag while Malaya snuck out to the stables and shooed the workers away.

The Jester joined her. They saddled two horses.

"Ready?"

"Not quite," The Jester peered outside toward the drawbridge. Unfortunately, several knights guarded the castle entrance. "Listen carefully, there's a secret bridge on the other side of the castle—servants use it at night—find it and cross over. Hide in the woods and wait for me."

"What are you going to do?"

The Jester looked back toward the knights, "I'm going to arm myself."

The knights had their back to the castle. They weren't expecting to be attacked from behind. They heard the jingle of bells and turned their heads in time to see a tight-clad jester—hat jingling—riding toward them.

They had no time to react. The Jester leaned over as far as he could, foot hooked in the stirrup of the saddle to keep from falling off. He snagged a sword right out of the sheath of a bewildered knight and rode past the other knights before they could react. With a head start, he rode into the woods, disappearing.

Malaya laughed in relief when he found her. She had safely crossed the secret bridge unseen. The two found the trail, and headed toward the Northern Mountain.

. . .

"What?" The king's face was red with rage. He had been bedridden, but upon hearing the news that the Jester had escaped, and his daughter was missing, he pushed himself from bed, and demanded the suitors meet him in the ballroom.

The three princes stood before him.

"My daughter has disappeared, I believe she may be going to the Northern Mountain. With my hand like this I cannot go after her myself. Whomever brings back the Princess Malaya safe to me shall take her as his wife."

"On my honor, I shall bring her back, my liege," Prince Galen declared.

"I shall return her safely to you," Prince Michael vowed.

Prince Kyran bowed silently.

"Go then, and beware the cursed prince."

Chapter Two

GENEVIEVE WAVERED BETWEEN consciousness and sleep. She came to several times in the carriage, but the Frozen Prince's icy gaze sent her retreating back to the darkness.

Eventually she woke to the sight of a castle outside the carriage window. It was as tall and imposing as its owner, half of the building was charred black by an ancient fire, the rest was coated in snow. The winter wind that chilled her told Genevieve that they had reached the mountain top. The thin air made her woozy.

When the carriage stopped, the Frozen Prince grabbed her and she struggled against him weakly. He pulled her into his arms and they exited the carriage.

Genevieve was hit by a blast of cold air. Snow flew all around her. She cried out and hugged herself against the cold, pressing herself against the prince's chest, despite her apprehension.

Warmth suddenly hit her. Genevieve realized she had passed out again. She found herself lying on a bed.

Looking up, she saw the prince feeding wood into a fireplace. The bedroom they occupied was covered in embroidered tapestries, the window was curtained. The fire was the only source of light.

The prince turned toward her.

Genevieve backed away, crawling backward over the bed. She felt her dress falling around her shoulders, revealing her cleavage. She quickly tried to pull it up. As she fumbled, the prince stepped onto the bed and pinned her down, his chilly hands grabbing her wrists and pressing them next to her hips.

"I *have* come as a suitor, m'lady," he said. He pressed his knees onto her wrists so that she was between his legs, held in place. Genevieve thrashed as his hand wandered to the already too-low collar of her dress.

"I'm not the princess!" she gasped.

The prince's hand hesitated, then journeyed to her head, where he removed her veil. Genevieve's thick hair tumbled free.

He chuckled.

"The chandelier girl."

Genevieve couldn't help but smirk. She *was* the chandelier girl. She had thwarted him *and* kept Malaya safe. She had won.

"Sorry to disappoint, your majesty."

He leaned forward, hands on either side of her head. Genevieve felt her heart begin to pound, and…something else, a strange tug in her stomach. There was something about the prince's gaze, his smell, even the gentle way he pinned her down.

A painful, yet pleasureful pang struck her abdomen as the prince touched her shoulder and traced her collarbone. Goosebumps blossomed over her skin and she inhaled sharply.

"I'm hardly disappointed," he whispered.

Genevieve began to tremble as his fingertips took the collar of her dress and began to pull it down. Cold air touched her nipples, making them pucker. Genevieve shut her eyes and turned her head away.

The prince hesitated.

"Have you never been touched by a man before?"

She didn't answer. She kept her eyes shut tight.

The weight of the prince left her body and Genevieve took a deep breath. She opened her eyes and watched as the prince left the room, shutting and locking the door behind him.

"Good to see you've returned safely," a voice caught the prince's attention as he entered the hallway. The Frozen Prince looked up at an old woman who stood hunched and dressed in black.

"Things did not go entirely as planned," he said.

The woman raised an eyebrow, "What happened? Was that not the princess you brought?"

"No. I need your eyes to see where she is."

The woman nodded and led him down the hall to another door, which opened to a spiral staircase. Down they went into a cellar filled with candles, bottles full of elixirs, talismans, and other items of the occult.

The woman sat herself down in a chair and drank

deep from a goblet on the table. After a moment, her eyes opened, now completely white.

"You have taken the daughter of a jester. He pursues her...wait..." the woman gasped, "the princess is with him! They journey up the mountain toward the castle."

"Are you sure?"

"Assuredly."

The woman leaned back and sighed, closing her eyes. When she opened them they were once again normal.

"Good," the prince said with a nod, "saves me the trouble of another kidnapping."

"Be careful, my prince. I sense a fire is coming."

The prince squeezed her shoulder. "Do not worry. Alert me if you see anything else." The prince turned and left.

The woman remained, staring at the burning candles.

"I can't believe I'm doing this. I've never been so far from the castle on my own before!" Malaya had not stopped talking about their act of rebellion for the entire journey. They had stopped for a rest, eating bread and cheese while the Jester tuned his lute.

"I'm with you," the performer protested.

"You're a jester. You don't count."

"The vote of confidence is inspiring."

"I'm just being realistic. Do you even know how to use that sword?"

"Yeah, the pointy end goes in the other guy."

Malaya rolled her eyes and shifted on the log she sat

on. Something skittered in the leaves near her, making her jump and move to the Jester's side.

"What? Scared of a little chipmunk?"

"I've never camped before. I'm nervous."

"Relax, it's just a little—it's coming this way!"

The two yelped and jumped up, running for the horses. After a moment of silence, they peeked over the backs of their horses.

"Princess? You alright?"

"Yes."

"I had the situation under control."

"I'm sure you did. Let's keep riding."

"Yes, good idea."

Genevieve gave up trying to get her gown buttoned up, and merely took it off, wearing only the slip underneath. The gown was too big to orchestrate an escape anyway. She tried the window first, but the room was too high up to escape that way.

Through the window pane she got a true sense of the desolate land she had entered. The snow storm seemed to go on for miles, covering the mountain peaks in white. She didn't even have shoes, if she managed to get out of the castle, how would she survive the trip back down the mountain?

Still, she couldn't stay here. Her heart pounded thinking of the prince returning, how he had pulled her dress away, how he stared at her, how she didn't entirely hate it...

Something stirred in her abdomen and she shook the

feeling away. Hopeless or not, she had to find a way out of this castle. Surely, she would be able to find boots and coat along the way.

Genevieve left the window and went to the door instead, studying the knob. Lock picking had not been one of the jester's lessons, unfortunately, but removing screws was easy enough.

After a brief search of the room, Genevieve found a letter opener that would do the trick. It was slow work, but she managed to free the screws with her fumbling tool. She wrenched the knob off the door and pushed it open.

The hallway was empty. Candles provided very little light to see by, and the windows were covered by tapestries and curtains. Genevieve approached one and yanked it from the wall, flooding the hallway with half-light from the window. Dust danced in the air. Genevieve studied the landscape outside, determining where she was inside the castle so that she could find her way outside. It was hard to tell for sure, so she picked a direction and started running.

Her bare feet padded against the stone floor and as she left the light of the window a feeling of dread seized her. The castle was freezing cold and her toes were becoming numb and blue. The shadows from the candles made the place seem haunted. She kept jumping at dark corners, expecting to see a frozen knight, or worse, the prince.

This was the castle that the rebels had attempted to burn down, where all those people had died. How many ghosts resided in its walls?

Genevieve finally came upon a flight of stairs and

followed them down to the ground floor. She entered a grand hallway where a door to the outside stood, waiting for her. Genevieve almost cheered for joy. As she started to run forward, a hand suddenly landed on her shoulder, and another clamped itself around her mouth as she started to scream.

"Easy! Easy!" A voice said. Genevieve turned her head to see an older gentleman holding her. He had salt and pepper hair, a scratchy beard, and narrow, kind eyes. "You can't go out there like that, I'll help you."

Genevieve calmed and ceased her fight. The man released her and smiled.

"There you are, come with me."

Having no alternative, Genevieve didn't question it. She followed the man. He took her hand and guided her down a side hall into another room.

The new room was a workshop filled with wooden carvings. In the middle was a table with a replica of a village. Other shelves held toys and animals. At the desk were a variety of supplies and carving tools.

Something clicked in Genevieve's memory.

"You're the toymaker. The one that disappeared."

The man nodded.

"Did you make all of these?"

"Yes. When I first came here the prince was just a child that wanted to play with toys," the man said, taking up a paintbrush and adding some detail to one of the houses on his model. "My wife had passed away, and my daughter was sick, so I agreed to work for him. Even now that my daughter has passed I still live here, making my little trinkets and running the estate as best I can."

"Is it true that there's a witch as well?" Genevieve walked around the room, studying all the toys. The craftsmanship was admirable.

"Yes, though I hardly see her. She tells the prince of the outside world, uses her powers to read the future for him."

"So, he didn't kidnap you?"

"No, he has never taken anyone against their will. We've had servants and cooks in the past but they were all compensated and free to leave. I don't know why he would take you. I've never seen him like this."

"Do you know how I can get out of here?"

"I can lend you some clothes and shoes, but it's a hard journey by yourself I'm afraid. The mountain top is in constant winter, and the climb down is dangerous unless you know the path."

"There must be some way—"

Their conversation was cut off by the sudden opening of the door. The prince walked in. Genevieve jumped in fright and the toymaker dropped his brush.

Genevieve didn't hesitate. She charged forward, crashing into the prince and using the momentum to run past him. She felt his cold hands on her arms and dress as he tried to seize her, but she kicked and punched her way free. She sprinted down the hall, back to the main foyer. She grabbed the handles of the main door and pulled it open with some difficulty. The wood was heavy and in no hurry to open.

She looked over her shoulder as she heard footsteps

coming for her. The Frozen Prince approached, but the Toymaker grabbed his sleeve, yelling and trying to hold him back. Genevieve pulled the door wide enough to squeeze through, and darted outside.

"What are you doing?" the Toymaker demanded, trying to stop the prince.

"This isn't your affair," the prince growled, trying to push him off.

"I can't believe this. Attacking another man's castle, stealing his daughter…"

"She is the daughter of a jester."

"She's not yours!"

The prince glared at him.

"Your heart may no longer beat, my prince, but your mind works just fine. Why would you do this?"

The prince did not answer. He pulled himself free of the older man's grasp and went to the door, pulling it open with ease. He saw Genevieve running into the storm. Two knights who stood guard at the door were going after her.

"Halt!" the prince ordered. "I'll handle her."

The wind bellowed against his cloak as he entered the storm.

Genevieve screamed in pain when her bare feet hit the snow and the cold wind lashed against her exposed skin. She held herself to no avail, running through the falling snow. This wasn't going to work. She would die out here before the hour was up.

Genevieve turned, giving in to the fact that she would have to return to the castle, but when she did, she saw only a wall of white. She couldn't have run more than ten yards, but the storm had already turned her around and hidden the castle from her.

Then a sound rumbled through the whistling storm. Genevieve stopped in her tracks, not moving, but the sound grew closer—the growling of some creature that had found her.

Genevieve carefully backed away. The thing followed. Genevieve could make out its shape in the storm, but not what it actually was. What kind of animal lived this far up the mountain in this constant storm?

Then, suddenly, the storm stopped. The snowflakes paused in the air, the wind died down. The creature stepped forward, and Genevieve could finally see it clearly. She didn't know what it was, it looked like a wingless gargoyle she had seen in grand churches. Its skin was white, and its eyes dark. It stayed low to the ground, growling at her.

Genevieve took a step back.

It charged.

Genevieve screamed and fell back, her arms flying up to shield her face as the creature hit her. She heard a scuffle in the snow and opened her eyes to see the prince standing over her. He seized the animal by the throat and tossed it into the snow. It scrambled and retreated, glaring at them over its shoulder.

The prince turned toward her, pulling off his cloak in a flourish of snowflakes. He lifted her and tightly wrapped the garment around her body. Genevieve started to shake.

"W-wh-what was that?"

"A creature designed by a witch to keep intruders away," he answered curtly. His hands were running over her thigh and shoulder, rubbing her to create heat. Genevieve trembled, her teeth chattering.

The castle reappeared and he carried her inside. It wasn't much warmer inside. Genevieve started to whimper. She felt the prince's arms tighten as he carried her through the halls back into his bedroom.

He placed her on the bed, and continued to rub, keeping some fabric between his hands and her body. He focused on her feet, and pulled a blanket over the cloak. Still she shivered.

"You need warm water. Stay here. *Don't move.*"

Genevieve jumped, but obeyed, too cold to attempt escape. She listened to the bustling of a fire being built and water being drawn. She pulled herself into a ball, trying to find some body heat.

She felt the blankets being pulled away, and tried to get them back, but firm hands took her wrists and pulled her up. She opened her eyes and saw that she was being guided into a connected washroom, where a bath had been drawn, embers beneath the tub warmed the water. The steam from the water renewed her blood flow.

She felt the hands pulling up the hem of her skirt.

"N-n-no!"

"I'm not looking," the prince said. Genevieve tried to push him away and undress herself, but, without his support her numb feet only caused her to collapse. The prince managed to wrap his arms around her, keeping her from hitting the floor.

His hands returned to her slip, pulling it up and over her head. Genevieve tried to cover herself as the prince lifted her off the floor. His hands brushed her body, bringing the return of the strange feeling in her stomach—the fearful pleasure. It was like the adrenaline she felt when she went to the top of a tower and looked directly down—exhilarating, dangerous.

Warm water covered her as the prince lowered her into the bath. Genevieve whimpered and sunk down into the tub, relaxing as began to warm up. She opened her eyes. The prince was still there, but he was purposely looking away.

He placed a towel on the floor next to her. "Dry yourself completely. When you're done, stay by the fire and use the blankets. Get some sleep."

Genevieve stared up at him, but he did not meet her gaze.

Why? Why go after her? She wasn't the princess.

What did he want?

Genevieve held her breath and slipped under the water, bringing life back into her cheeks and frozen nose. She felt so tired, too tired for questions. She was trapped here, and with that monster patrolling the mountain, the chance of a rescue was completely gone—however small it had been before.

With a sigh of defeat, Genevieve sank back into the water.

Malaya groaned. They had been riding for hours, and every part of her was sore. The air had become more cold and thin as they neared the mountain top. Snow was falling around them.

"Jester, can we stop?"

"We can't waste time. Bear it a little longer. With all this snow we'll lose the trail."

"Just a quick break then? I hear running water. We can let the horses drink and stretch our limbs."

"Alright, but don't dawdle."

They dismounted and led the horses through the trees until they reached a small creek. The Jester broke the ice out of the way so the horses could drink.

"Watch the horses. I need to relieve myself," he said, wandering into the trees for privacy. Malaya found a log to sit herself down on.

A twig snapped behind her.

Malaya jumped up and spun around. A third horse appeared in the trees, riding it was Prince Galen.

"Princess, thank heavens," Prince Galen said, dismounting.

"Prince Galen…you followed me?"

"Your father sent all three of us to find you and bring you home."

"No, I can't, I have to save my friend."

"Majesty, your father is ill with worry, I am taking you back." Prince Galen stepped forward and grabbed Malaya's wrist. When she tried to pull away he bent over, grabbed her waist, and hauled her up over his shoulder.

"Galen! Stop!"

"I'm sorry but you're forcing my hand."

"My friend needs me! If you help us…I'll marry you."

"Your father has already promised your hand to the man that brings you home."

"He what?"

Galen pulled her off his shoulder and placed her on his horse, but before he could mount, something crashed over his head, sending him crumbling to the ground. The Jester stood behind him, holding his broken lute.

"Are you okay?" the Jester helped Malaya off the horse. "What's he doing here?"

Malaya glared at the unconscious prince, her voice dripped with poison. "Apparently the king said that if he brought me back I could be his wife." Malaya gave his body a kick to the ribs. "I can't believe this!"

"What?" the Jester asked, confused.

"He put me over his shoulder like a bag of meal! As if marriage is fair trade! I am not an object, Jester, I will not be treated this way!"

Malaya bent down and pulled Galen's sword from its sheath.

"What are you doing?" the Jester's mouth dropped in shock.

"Taking control. If Galen is here, then the other two will be coming as well. Come on, let's go." Malaya mounted her horse, and secured the sword to her waist.

"As you wish, your majesty," the Jester said, sincere respect in his voice. Malaya gave him a grateful smile, and they continued the ride.

Genevieve lay on the floor, drying her hair by the fireplace. She had wrapped herself in blankets while her dress dried next to the fire. As tired as she was, she was having trouble getting any sleep.

She kept thinking of the prince, his hands on her body, his eyes staring at her.

Her stomach gave a jolt, and she shook her head, trying to cast the thoughts away.

The door was suddenly pushed open and she jumped in surprise. The Frozen Prince entered, carrying a tray. Genevieve's eyes locked on it, smelling the food there. She hadn't realized how hungry she was. He looked at her with a hard, disapproving expression and set the tray on the floor.

A bowl of thick stew sat on the tray, with a chunk of bread and a glass of wine. Genevieve took it with trembling hands and sipped at the broth eagerly. It burned the roof of her mouth, but warmed her stomach wonderfully.

"So, what was your plan, exactly?" the prince leaned against the fireplace, towering over her. "To run away through a snow-covered mountain with no clothes or shoes and survive?"

Genevieve didn't look at him.

"Is your presence here really so terrible?"

Now Genevieve did look up. "You've no right to take someone against their will."

His expression darkened.

Genevieve looked away and ate her bread.

Then he was upon her. Genevieve yelped as he grabbed her shoulders and forced her back onto the floor. Genevieve struggled to keep the blankets over her body, but he grabbed her wrists and pinned her down. She felt them slip against her skin, threatening to fall away. She didn't dare struggle.

"I have taken nothing from you."

Genevieve trembled. She could feel the blankets, still slipping...

His face was close, too close. He leaned down to her chest. The blanket fell away. Genevieve's face flared with heat. The prince sighed.

"You're heart beats so fast. You get so much warmer when you think you've been compromised..." His face brushed over her chest, onto the swell of her breast—lips and nose touching the flushed skin there. Genevieve started to pant, her chest rising up higher into his face.

"I do hope you'll forgive my intrusion," he whispered, "I truly don't wish to hurt you, but you're so warm, I can practically hear your blood rushing."

His lips touched her nipple, and Genevieve jumped, finally pulling her hands out of his soft grip and pulling the blankets back over herself.

She felt strange, her thighs were wet, her stomach was doing flips. She couldn't meet his gaze.

"I'm sorry," he said, rising.

Genevieve stared at him, silent. It wasn't right, no, but...

"I'm sorry," he said again, turning away. He went to the door and reached for the knob, but his hand only met air.

He cast a look at her over his shoulder.

Genevieve couldn't stop herself. She started to laugh,

deep belly laughs that hurt her ribs. She clutched her sides and gasped for air. He stared at her with bewilderment.

"I keep thwarting you at every turn," she finally managed to speak between giggles, "and I'm just a laundry maid!"

He glared, but she only laughed harder.

"Then, perhaps, you should sleep in the laundry room tonight."

Genevieve caught her breath and wiped the water from her eyes. "Don't be rude. You kidnapped me, the least you can do is let me sleep in a bed."

"I should put you in the dungeon for your trickery."

Genevieve stood and went to the bed, crawling under the covers. "Too late."

"You are a strange creature."

"We'll get along just fine, then," Genevieve replied. He stared at her a moment longer, shook his head, as if giving up on a thought, and left the room.

Genevieve smiled and settled in, but when she closed her eyes she still saw his face. His crystalline eyes, the way his lips touched her nipple, making it harden...

Her hand wandered to the breast he had kissed, and she squeezed her nipple between her fingers, making her vagina flare and moisten. She sighed, remembering his hands on her body, pinning down her wrists.

While one hand messaged her breast, the other went between her legs. She rolled her clitoris under her finger, quickening her breath. She imagined the prince coming back, holding her against the bed, kissing other parts of her body.

It was too absurd. She had grown too wild. She had outwitted the most feared royal in the land and the best part, the thing that made it all so funny...

She *wanted* him.

Genevieve played with herself until she was too sleepy to continue. She built herself up to a soft release, enjoying her wet folds and the euphoria that filled her brain as the day finally caught up with her and she fell into an untroubled sleep.

Chapter Three

PRINCE GALEN GROANED AS HE CAME
to, finding himself alone in the wilderness. The
princess and the Jester had fled.

No, not entirely alone.

Prince Kyran stood a few feet away, studying the
footprints in the snow. When Galen stirred, Kyran stood
up and approached him.

"Kyran, what are you—" Before Galen could finish,
Kyran raised his sword, and brought it down on his head.

"What happened?" the king demanded.

Prince Michael half carried Galen into the castle,
while servants rushed forward to aid him. Galen was badly
injured, and Michael was not much better.

"Kyran attacked, my lord," Michael gasped, collapsing
into a chair. "He ambushed me, and when I came to, I
tried to get back down the mountain. That was when I
found Galen, almost dead. I can only assume Kyran

attacked him as well. No doubt he wants no competition for the princess."

The king groaned. The queen squeezed his shoulder in an attempt to comfort him.

"A kidnapper ahead, a killer behind, and only a jester at her side. What will happen to our Malaya?"

The mountain was becoming steeper, the sky threatening a storm. The horses Malaya and the jester rode were growing weary. They pushed on.

"Are you alright, m'lady?" the Jester asked.

"Perfectly."

"You're very quiet."

"I don't need to speak to convey my health, Jester. Please focus on the journey, we need to figure out how we're going to get to Genevieve when we arrive at the castle."

"I'm hoping we can be...diplomatic," the Jester said.

"Not without giving myself up, I'm afraid. No, we need to be stealthy, and forceful."

"There's only two of us."

"I can count, sir."

"Yes, of course your ladyship, forgive me."

Malaya sighed. "I'm sorry for being short with you, I'm still just...angry from before."

"No need to apologize, my lady. Really you're quite tall."

Malaya cast him a glare, in doing so she spotted something over his shoulder, hiding in the snowy brush. "Someone's there!"

Just as she shouted the warning, a group of men jumped out from the trees, surrounding them in a tight circle. The horses neighed and bucked. Malaya was thrown from her horse. She grabbed for her sword, but one of the men stopped her, tossing the weapon away and pinning her to the snow.

The Jester reached for his weapon as well but was quickly overpowered and pulled from his horse.

"Get off, you scoundrel!" Malaya screeched.

"Well, well, you're a pretty one," the man said, smiling.

"Don't you *dare* touch her!" the Jester warned, fighting against his captures.

"Well I *was* going to rob you two, but I think I'll ask you to marry me instead," the man grinned down at Malaya. The others laughed.

Malaya glared at him. He was a lean man with an athletic body, tall riding boots, and a thick poncho to protect him from the weather.

"Are you going to give me a hard time if I let you up?"

Malaya thought of Genevieve as she answered, "Yes."

The man's smile widened. "Good."

He stood and pulled Malaya to her feet. "Never mind, boys, doesn't look like they have much of value."

"How about the horses?" One asked

"What do you think, little miss? Spare a horse?" he asked, grin growing wider.

Malaya raised her hand and struck him across the face. "I am *quite done* with men like you. You think you can just take whatever you want, don't you? Even people?

Well, I am the Princess Malaya, heir to the central throne, and I say it ends now!" Her knee came up, meeting her assailant squarely between the legs. All the men froze. Their leader made a strained sound and collapsed. Malaya marched forward and grabbed her sword from the ground. The other men drew their own weapons.

"Malaya, don't!" the Jester warned.

"You *will* let us pass!"

"Yes, we will," the leader spoke up, carefully rising. One of his group helped him to his feet. "But not before you dine with us." The grin returned.

Malaya stared at him, mouth agape. "Are you mad?"

"Madly in love." He took his hat off and bowed to her. "I do apologize, your majesty. Please do us the honor of supping at our camp."

"Dining with thieves? I think not. Besides, we have no time, we are on a rescue mission."

This time the leader frowned, raising an eyebrow. "Rescue? You must share this tale. I insist you eat with us, no point traveling the mountain on an empty stomach."

The Jester approached, placing a reassuring hand on Malaya's shoulder. "These men might prove useful, m'lady. They could show us how to navigate the mountain."

Malaya lowered her sword. "Very well, but no funny business."

The men laughed.

"Us? Funny business? I make no promises."

Malaya and the Jester were guided off the trail and into the woods. The band of thieves led them to an ancient road, and the group followed it to a ghost town. Malaya frowned.

"Was this a village?"

"Aye," the leader said, "after the revolution the villagers left, so we've made use of it. No one comes this far up the mountain."

"Why?"

"Because of the *curse*." The men laughed.

"The Frozen Prince," Malaya said.

The leader nodded. "Nothing we can't handle of course. We rob the caravans and he stays in his castle. Sometimes he sends knights after us, but we're too smart for them, ain't that right, boys?"

The group gave a cheer and everyone filed into a building that was once an inn. The large open space held many long tables. In the middle of the room was a roaring fire where a boar was being roasted. The men took their seats and mead was passed around.

"Right this way, m'lady. You'll be my guest of honor."

Malaya rolled her eyes, but complied, making sure the Jester was at her side. They went to the table at the head of the room and took a seat. The leader removed his hat.

"Your ladyship will have probably heard of me. They call me the Bandit of the North."

Malaya perked up, recognizing the title. "I do! You've pulled off great robberies and jail breaks! I've heard about you!"

The Bandit smiled proudly.

The boar was cut and the meat was passed around.

Malaya and the Jester fell into their meal eagerly. The fire was warm, as was the mead.

"Thank you for your hospitality," the Jester said.

"My pleasure, but don't forget our bargain. You must enlighten me on this rescue mission and why it's being led by a princess."

"My friend has been kidnapped by the Frozen Prince."

At the mention of the prince, the crowd fell silent, listening in. The Bandit's smile disappeared.

"He tried to kidnap me, but she took my place. I'm going to the castle to get her back."

"That is a...noble, but perilous errand, m'lady," the Bandit said.

"I know, but no one else would go."

"Why?" he asked, confused.

"She's only a laundry maid."

He laughed. "And you would risk your life for a laundry maid?"

"No, I would risk my life for my best friend."

The Bandit's smile turned into something like admiration. Malaya felt a blush caress her cheeks and quickly looked away.

"We would be most grateful for any help you might give us," the Jester cut in.

The Bandit leaned back and stroked his chin thoughtfully. "I'll help, but for a price."

"I'm *not* marrying you."

He laughed. "Nor do I expect you to, but surely a princess has good rewards to offer? Some jewels? A few pardons, perhaps?"

Malaya nodded slowly. "Yes, I think something could be done, certainly. But we need help getting up the mountain, and sneaking into the castle."

"You may have some difficulty with that. The land is guarded by unnatural creatures, and guards stand at the door."

"I'll make it worth your while."

The Bandit smiled ruefully. "No amount of money is worth the lives of my men."

"I ask for no one's lives, only what help you can offer."

"I can get you up the mountain safely. From there we'll have to see." The Bandit rose, bowed his head, and walked away. Malaya watched as he circled the room, speaking to his men.

"Very well handled, your majesty," the Jester said.

"Well, I didn't take all those diplomacy classes for nothing," Malaya said, though she felt incredibly nervous and out of her element. With food in her belly she wanted nothing more than to sleep.

The Bandit must have noticed this, for when he made it back to their table he gave her a teasing grin. "You look like you're about to pass out in your plate."

"I'm perfectly fit, thank you. When do we leave?"

"In the morning."

Malaya opened her mouth to protest.

"Now, princess, mark me. It's no good climbing the mountain at night. It's far too late to continue the journey. Rest tonight, and you'll be fresh and ready tomorrow."

Malaya looked at the Jester. "But Genevieve..."

A pained look crossed the Jester's face. "I know, but

he's right. We'd fall or freeze once the sun has gone. We've no choice."

The Bandit perked up. "You can sleep in my room!"

Malaya glared at him. The Jester quickly stepped between them. "It's a good idea, Malaya, get some rest. I'll guard the door."

"Very well."

The Bandit showed them upstairs and led them to his room. It was cozy and warmed by a small stove. Malaya went happily to the bed where soft rabbit pelts blanketed her. The Bandit watched her from the doorway.

"Alright, your ladyship?"

Malaya was already dozing. The Jester closed the door and gave him a pointed look.

"What do you think it would take to win the princess's heart?" the Bandit mused.

"A title, lack of a criminal record, her father's approval," the Jester said testily.

"Ah, not too hopeless then, eh?"

"Can you really get us up the mountain?"

"Of course! Don't you trust me?" He grinned. "I know all the safe paths. But I wonder if I shouldn't help you get the princess back home instead. It isn't right putting the poor thing in danger like this."

The Jester considered this offer. "You're right, but I couldn't do that to her. She broke me out of the dungeon. She's been through too much today to turn back now. But," the Jester met the Bandit's eyes, "she does need protection."

"I'll stay by her side, don't worry." He took the Jester's

hand and gave it a firm shake. "So, a dungeon, huh? Do you need to join my merry band?"

"After the king gets hold of me? Perhaps."

The Bandit chuckled and returned to his men. The Jester sat on the floor and rested against the wall, but sleep was far away.

A sound from under the bed woke her. Genevieve wasn't sure how long she had been asleep, but dawn was peeking through the curtains on the window. The fire had died down to embers.

The sound came again—a low whisper. Genevieve rose and fetched her slip from where it hung by the fireplace. It was dry and warm now. She dressed then went to her belly and peered under the bed. A face stared back at her. Genevieve jumped in surprise.

"Come with me child, hurry." The face belonged to an old woman.

"Are you the witch?"

"Yes, take my hand, before he comes back." The Witch reached her hand forward. Genevieve took it, and she was pulled under the bed.

After a moment of blindness, Genevieve blinked, and found herself lying on the floor of a new room. There was a fireplace in the middle of this room, with a cauldron sitting on top of it. The walls were lined with shelves that contained potions, herbs, books, and several oddities.

Genevieve pushed herself to her feet. "How did you do that?"

"I told you, I'm the witch," the old woman smiled.

"Why help me?"

"I can see into the future, child, and your coming here has pushed the prince down a dangerous path. A fire is coming."

"I don't even know why I'm here. He knew I was a servant girl!"

"I confess I'm not sure myself. But the point is, you must leave." The Witch sat down at her table and began to crush various herbs with a mortar and pestle. Genevieve sat across from her, watching with interest.

"I had a vision, several months ago, and it has plagued me since. In this vision I saw my prince, sitting alone in the ice, holding his frozen heart in his hand. His eyes had gone vacant, as if he had no soul within."

The Witch tipped the ingredients into a vial, then added a strange liquid.

"What does it mean?" Genevieve asked.

The Witch sighed tiredly, whispering something to the jar. It began to glow, casting shadows on her face. "Did you know that every witch knows when she is going to die? As she ages it is a premonition that becomes apparent to her. I know when I am going to die, I've seen it looming, like a tower on the horizon that gets bigger and bigger."

The Witch pointed to an hourglass on her shelf. Genevieve studied it, for there was something unusual about it. It was filled with black sand falling at a strange rate, far more slowly than a normal hourglass.

"I know how much time I have and when I am gone the prince will be alone."

"Is that hourglass…is that your life?"

The Witch nodded. "The prince saved me when I was scheduled to be hanged for my witchcraft. He came to me in my cell when he was still a young man. Imagine my surprise as I sat in my cell during one of the hottest days of the year, and snow starts to fall. It was a relief I cannot express. He broke the bars with his ice, and took me away. He saved me from the noose, and I have struggled to repay him since that day.

"I thought I saw my chance today. I saw that the princess Malaya had come of age. I told him to befriend her, to bring her to the castle and create an alliance between our kingdoms. I wanted the prince to know another, a friend, anything that might melt his poor heart, and keep him from loneliness. Why he decided to *steal* her, I don't know."

Genevieve frowned, deep in thought. The Toymaker and Witch's stories of the prince revealed him as someone tragic but kind. So why such a sudden change in personality?

Something else was going on.

"This is a potion that will help you sneak through the castle," the Witch interrupted her thoughts, handing over the vial, which had ceased to glow. "You must escape, there are others coming for you."

"There are?"

"Your father."

Genevieve smiled, eyes widening in surprise. As she reached for the vial, a heavy pounding suddenly shook the door. They both jumped.

"Quick! Drink it and hide under my bed."

Without question, Genevieve gulped down the contents of the vial, and crawled under the bed as the Witch answered the door. The prince charged in.

"The girl is gone. Find her."

"Y-yes," the Witch went to her chair and looked into a crystal ball.

Genevieve watched from her hiding place, but something was wrong. She could feel something happening to her body. What was this spell? She shut her eyes in fear.

The ground shuddered beneath her. Genevieve's eyes snapped open, and she realized that something was very different, and very wrong. She could see the prince's pacing feet, but they were huge. Genevieve moved and realized she could stand upright under the bed. The potion had shrunk her. She stood about four inches tall.

"I'm sorry," the Witch spoke, "it's too vague . . ."

"Keep looking, find her."

The prince turned to leave, and Genevieve saw her chance. She ran along the wall, staying under furniture and out of sight. When the prince opened the door again, she slipped through behind him. She waited as he walked down the hall and turned the corner, then began to run down the opposite wall.

As she did, a hand suddenly came down and seized her.

Malaya cried out as she jerked awake. Her sleep was fitful and full of nightmares, thoughts of Genevieve in danger and an unease of her situation. She kept waking, not knowing what time it was and sometimes not remembering *where* she was.

There was a soft knock at the door.

"Come in," she said, thinking it was the Jester.

The Bandit opened the door, carrying a candle. Malaya stiffened. "Not you."

He paused in the doorway. "I'm sorry. Your friend fell asleep and I heard you cry out. Is everything alright?"

"Just having trouble sleeping," Malaya said, rubbing her eyes. The Bandit entered, but left the door open. He placed the candle on her bedside table and gathered up a blanket which had been kicked to the floor. He spread it over her body.

"Would you like me to build you a fire?" he asked.

"No, the blankets are enough," Malaya said, sitting up to fix her pillow. "I'm sure you think me quite spoiled."

"Used to the finer things perhaps, but 'spoiled' seems a bit harsh." The Bandit sat on the floor, leaning his back against her bed. "Should I be a king with plenty of money and fine possessions I should want to spoil my daughter too."

"Do you have a daughter?"

"No, no, I wouldn't dare. You might have noticed a shortage of women in our little community. Most of these men are on the run and can never see their wives and children again."

"You're all criminals then?"

"Technically, yes."

"Technically?"

"Well, I would never take in murderers or anyone like that. Most of these men are thieves, or in debt, some poachers. Mostly their crimes are that they're poor and desperate."

"And you?"

"I am rich in my heart, never desperate, and I am most certainly a master thief."

"I am...surprised by your high spirits," Malaya admitted. She allowed herself to slip back down under the blankets, comforted by the Bandit's presence.

"I always laugh in the face of adversity."

"Even when things are serious and everything is hopeless?"

"Especially then."

Malaya sighed and released one of her hands from the blankets, letting it dangle over the side of the bed. "I envy you then, for I am quite afraid."

She felt his hand close over hers. "You've come far for someone so afraid."

"Yes, indeed I have."

"Your friend must be quite special." He pressed his thumb into her palm. Malaya smiled secretly in the dark.

"She is. She risked her life for me. We've been friends since childhood. But..."

"What?"

"To be honest, it's more than that. I left the castle for selfish reasons as well. Not just her rescue."

"Oh?"

"I...I wanted to escape my betrothal. Three suitors came to our castle and I was more afraid of them than running off into the wilderness. The excuse to run away and find Genevieve was to escape matrimony as well. I feel that I have been quite used in my stature, especially now, knowing that my marriage can be made as a bargaining tool, never mind what I want." Malaya gritted her teeth. "I get upset just thinking about it."

"I don't think that's selfish. I've never known anyone to happily go into an arranged marriage. However, there is always the chance that it might work out in the end."

"I honestly don't know what will happen when I return. I want no part of the ordeal. Just thinking of it makes me angry."

"Make them earn it then," the Bandit of the North said. "In the end, nothing can happen until you say 'I do'. Just use the energy you had when you kicked me in the family jewels and put them all to their knees."

Malaya laughed. "My manners say I should apologize for that."

"No, don't you dare."

"I won't, ever."

"Good. Will you do as I advise?"

"Yes, I think I will."

"Then I have a difficult challenge ahead of me. I think my greatest robbery will be stealing your heart."

"Stay on the floor, thief."

"Of course, princess."

They remained that way, holding hands, while Malaya drifted back to sleep. The Bandit stayed with her, watching the candle slowly melt down. She had no more nightmares and made no further sounds.

• • •

A hand reached in and grabbed Genevieve, pulling her out of the pocket she had been placed inside of.

"You scared me to death," she told the Toymaker, clutching his fingers as he lifted her up.

"Sorry, but better me finding you than a misguided foot."

They were back in the toymaker's room. He placed her on the table with the village replica. Genevieve walked through it, almost the perfect size. She ran her hands over the fine details that her larger eyes had missed before. The Toymaker began digging through the shelves, looking for something.

"This is beautiful."

"Thank you. It is my village, where I lived many years ago with my family."

"I'm sorry about what happened to them."

"Thank you. This music box was actually my daughter's." He produced a small wooden box and opened it. A dancing girl unfolded from it, and spun along to the soft music it played. "Her name was M'kala, gone far too young." He set the box on the table and, pulling out a screwdriver, began to remove the wooden girl.

"Oh, don't do that!"

"It's alright, I can fix absolutely anything, it's quite a talent, actually. This will make the perfect hiding place to sneak you out." He turned the box toward her, and Genevieve climbed in. As he shut the lid, her platform went down, allowing her to sit inside comfortably. There was a small keyhole that she could look through.

"I'll make an excuse and take you down the mountain as far as I can."

"Thank you," Genevieve whispered through the keyhole. She felt her box being lifted, then stop again as the Toymaker carried it out of the room. After a moment cold snuck into the box through the keyhole. Genevieve looked through and saw that they were outside, she watched as they walked over the castle grounds toward a large stable.

Her view was suddenly blocked. Someone stepped in front of the Toymaker. She shivered at the sound of the prince's voice.

"Where are you going?"

"I have a gift to deliver," the Toymaker answered calmly. He started to move again, but the prince placed a hand on his shoulder, frost crept from his hand over the toymaker's coat.

"Where is she?"

"I don't know. I just wanted to visit my daughter."

"Even your deep sentimentality doesn't force you into the cold at such an hour."

Genevieve slid to the back of the box as it was forcefully jostled.

"Give that back!" the Toymaker shouted.

"You will die in this storm. Go back inside, and I will return it to you." The prince gripped the Toymaker's arm and forced him back toward the castle. Genevieve curled up, trying not to get tossed around.

"You need to let that girl go," the Toymaker snapped.

"I don't have time to explain the importance of this to you. *Where is she?*"

"Why do you want her? Have you gotten so lonely you would kidnap a poor girl?"

A venomous silence fell between them.

"After all we've been through," the prince said, "do you really think me so cruel? I did everything I could for M'kala. I wept beside you when she died. Do you really think I took this girl without good reason?"

He shoved the Toymaker away and stormed off.

Genevieve hugged her knees, being bounced around unceremoniously by the prince's angry retreat. Behind them, she could hear the toymaker crying.

The walk finally ended, and the box went still as it was set down. She tried to look through the keyhole, but the lid was opening, and her platform was rising. Genevieve froze.

They were back in the prince's bedroom. He didn't notice her at first, only stared off, listening to the music.

Genevieve carefully began to twirl, hoping that he wouldn't realize that she was real. She stood on her toes and spun, just as her father taught her.

The Frozen Prince stood at the window and opened it, staring outside until the song finally wound down, ending with a click. Genevieve froze.

"You're a beautiful dancer," he said.

Genevieve blushed and jumped off the music box, but there was nowhere to go. She had been placed on a dresser, and the fall would cripple her. Giving up, she turned to the prince as he walked toward her.

The half-light enhanced his pale skin and sharp eyes. He was frighteningly beautiful. A few misguided snowflakes drifted through the window, dancing around his gaze.

"Is this the witch's work?" he asked, reaching forward. Genevieve stiffened as his large fingers took her tiny hands and gave her a small spin.

"No," she said quickly, not wanting to get anyone in trouble. "I'm magic too."

He smiled, amused. He touched her dress. "Go on then, put yourself back to normal."

Genevieve tried to push his fingers away, but he kept running them over her tiny body, squeezing her waist and touching her hair. She ducked away.

"I don't want to."

"Very well." His hand cupped her, picking her up. Genevieve gasped, falling back. She hugged his thumb to keep from falling. He carried her out of the room, cupping her to his chest. They walked down the hallway, heading downstairs.

"Why am I here?" she asked.

"Because I made a mistake."

"No…you knew I was a servant girl. You didn't seem surprised when you found out."

"Is that how you define yourself? Servant girl? Princess? Does it matter at all?"

"To some." Genevieve suddenly gasped as her body gave a jolt. She realized she was growing again. The prince shifted her from his hand to his arms, continuing to carry her as she grew to twenty inches, then forty.

"You also dropped a chandelier upon me, and took the place of your friend. I care not for stature."

Genevieve's body ached as it reached four feet, then five. The prince carried her down the stairs. They reached the lowest level of the castle. Genevieve realized it was the dungeon.

"Why are we here?"

"Because things are about to get serious and the dungeons are safe."

"Safe...from what?"

"You'll see soon enough, for now we must wait."

Chapter Four

THE BANDIT, THE JESTER, AND MALAYA struggled up the mountain. The trail was steep and they had reached the top, caught in a snow storm. The horses were too skittish in the magical storm, so had been left behind in the Bandit's village.

Malaya slipped and the Bandit grabbed her, keeping her upright. She gripped his arm, allowing him to keep her in his grip so their pace wouldn't slow.

"It's a constant storm," the Bandit explained, "it's how you know you've reached the Frozen Prince's land."

"And you said there's a…creature that roams these woods?"

"Aye, if you wander too close to the castle."

Malaya grabbed the hilt of her sword.

"Don't worry, I'll get you as close to the castle as I can."

"I thank you for getting us this far," Malaya said, "the other trail would have taken us days."

"Anything to stay in your company, m'lady."

Malaya rolled her eyes, but hid a smile as well. As a princess no one had dared flirt with her so openly, and she found that she was enjoying it. She liked how her heart fluttered and how sincere he seemed. No formalities or awkwardness, just fun.

Well, as much fun as one could have on a desolate snow-covered mountain.

There was a crash from above. The Jester looked up to see a man jump from the trees. With a cry, he dodged the attack. The Bandit jumped in front of Malaya, going for his sword. Before he could draw, the assailant's blade entered his shoulder.

"No!" Malaya screamed.

The Jester looked up. It was Prince Kyran.

The prince pulled his sword from the Bandit and slashed at the Jester with his blade. The Jester swiftly drew his own, defending himself. The princess took the Bandit in her arms. She took the scarf from his neck and pressed it against the wound.

The Bandit grabbed her arms and pushed her on up the trail. "Run, princess!" he hissed. Malaya turned to check on the Jester. She watched in amazement as the Jester held his own against Kyran. His expression was hard, his stance professional. He actually managed to lock the hilt of Kyran's sword on his own and force the man to his knees. Malaya ran forward, pulling out the sword she stole from Galen and holding it to Kyran's neck.

Kyran froze.

"Back away."

Kyran dropped his sword and slowly stood, arms up.

Malaya kept her sword pointed. "Get out of here! Go!" she ordered.

Kyran didn't move.

Malaya charged him, readying her sword for a swing. Kyran jumped in shock and retreated, dodging her blow. He kept backing away, but paused again, and looked at the Jester.

"No man short of knighthood has ever held his own against me in battle. Who are you?"

"Nobody. Just a jester, a silly old fool."

Kyran stared a moment longer, then turned back down the path. Malaya kept her blade pointed after him until he was down the trail and out of sight.

She sighed and dropped the sword. "Why are these things so damn heavy?" she demanded, turning back to the two men.

The Jester helped the Bandit to his feet, checking the wound. "It's not too bad. We should rest a moment and get it properly bandaged."

Malaya nodded and led the way. They stepped off the path, into the trees, where the snow was not hitting them so harshly. The Jester pulled out his knapsack and hitched his blanket to a tree branch, building a makeshift lean-to which would shield them from the storm. They cleared some snow and the Jester went to work on a fire while Malaya tended to the Bandit's wound.

She carefully peeled the clothes away from his shoulder. She wasn't used to such serious wounds, but her adventures with Genevieve in tree climbing, racing, and practice sword battles led to many visits to the nurse, so she had an idea of what to do.

She produced a handkerchief and cleaned the wound as best she could. The Bandit had some spare cloth, and she pressed this against the wound, before tying up a tourniquet with her shoelaces, then finishing the whole thing off by wrapping it with the scarf.

"I'm going to patrol the area," the Jester said, "make sure Kyran isn't trying to double back. You two rest a moment. I'll be right back."

"Be careful!" Malaya called. The Jester gave her a salute and left the lean-to.

"Are you alright?" she asked, turning back to the Bandit. "How does that feel?"

"Wonderful when you're doing it."

"Will you take this seriously? You could have been killed!"

"Nah, I would never do that to you, dear princess."

Malaya studied him, trying to see if he was joking. He had warm, green eyes that reflected the firelight when he smiled.

"I can't believe you chased off that man, that was amazing," he said.

"Was it?" Malaya said nonchalantly, pretending to scrape blood from her nails.

He touched her cheek with his fingers, bringing her gaze back to his face. "Are you sure you won't marry me?" The Bandit grinned at her.

"Oh, stop with that marrying nonsense."

"Why? I mean it."

"No, you don't."

"But I do."

Malaya studied him incredulously. "Yeah, you, the murderous villain stalking us in the woods, *and* the cursed prince."

The Bandit frowned, sympathy graced his expression. "That person who attacked us is a suitor?"

"Oh yes, a *prince* who's trying to bring me back so he can force me to marry him."

"I'm sorry, Malaya."

Malaya smirked. "Are we on first name basis now?"

His smile returned. "Well, my name is Roland and I won't force you into anything."

"You are the first to not try and stop me on this crusade."

"I wouldn't dare!" he laughed. "Not. after what I've seen you do."

Malaya smiled, finally relaxing her shoulders and lowing her guard.

"But I would still like to ask." He leaned forward then, and hesitated only centimeters from her face. When Malaya didn't pull away, he pressed his lips against hers, briefly but tenderly. Malaya blinked in surprise. His lips were soft, and he smelled of leather and freshly cut wood.

It was then that the Jester returned. "How's the patient?"

"I'm fine," Roland said, quickly pulling away. "It's just a scratch."

"Let me know when you're ready to leave then, we can't stay out in this storm."

Roland nodded in agreement and rose. They kicked out the fire and found their way back to the trail. This time Malaya held on to the Bandit, bracing him against the howling wind. They all had their weapons drawn now, ready for attack.

The party almost whooped for joy when the frame of the castle became visible through the storm. Malaya beamed and quickened her pace. "Finally, we made it."

"Stay low, we need to find a way to sneak inside," the Jester said.

A growl made them all stop in their tracks. It sounded like no animal they had heard before and the creature that made it was something between human and beast. It stalked toward them, growling its warning.

"Go on then," Roland said, stepping forward and holding his sword aloft. "This one's on me."

"What?" The Jester turned on him, "you've got a bloody hole in you."

"It's fine, I have to redeem myself in front of the lady."

"Or we could *all* fight it," Malaya said pointedly.

"You're a much smarter strategist than I, princess," Roland said.

"Just ignore him and circle it," the Jester instructed. They did so, flanking the creature as it continued to growl and hiss. Roland made the first strike, charging forward. The Jester came in from behind. The creature snarled and dodged both their attacks. As the swords came down it leaped into the air to tackle Roland, claws tearing through his clothes and into his skin. Malaya screamed.

The Jester took advantage of Roland's distress and

approached the creature from behind. It had Roland pinned, trying to get its jaw around his throat. The Jester raised his sword and methodically stabbed the blade into the creature's back, directly into its heart. With a death cry the creature rolled away and curled in on itself.

Roland struggled to his feet, panting. Claw marks decorated his chest, and the blood stained his torn shirt. As the Jester and Malaya approached him, however, Roland suddenly froze, a look of fear crossing his face. He was staring at something behind Malaya's shoulder.

"Watch out!"

Malaya turned and saw a shadowy figure standing over her—like a dark ghost in a flowing cloak. Before she could even scream, the shadow fell over her, wrapping her in the ethereal folds of its body. She and the specter disappeared, sword clattering to the stones.

"No!" the Jester ran forward, searching the snow. But Malaya was gone.

A shout caught their attention and they looked up to see the frozen guard running towards them. Roland jumped forward and shoved the Jester into the nearby brush.

"What are you doing?"

"They'll follow me! Get to the castle and find them! Find the girls!" With that, Roland ran into the forest. The frozen knights ran after him, passing the Jester's hiding spot.

"Do you know who you are?" the Frozen Prince asked, staring down at Genevieve.

Genevieve nodded. The prince stared, making her stomach flutter. She had to look away.

"When I was a boy a curse fell on me, freezing my heart." He stepped toward her. Genevieve stepped away, but her back met the cold stone wall of the dungeon. "In the stories my mother read me, it was always a royal kiss that would break the curse." He leaned toward her, hands resting on either side of her shoulders.

A familiar pang hit her stomach, and Genevieve felt her cheeks grow warm. The prince rested his fingertips on one of her cheeks, soaking in the warmth.

"Is that why you tried to take Malaya?" she whispered. "To break the curse?"

"Luckily for her, I don't believe in fairy tales. This curse is what keeps me alive. If it broke, my heart would beat, blood would flow, and I would die of my wound."

"Then why?" Genevieve asked. His fingers wandered from her check, down her neck, to her shoulder, where he slipped off the sleeve of her dress.

"Because, I hated you." His hands seized her arms, gripping tightly. Genevieve jolted in fear. "From the Witch's crystal ball, I watched you, laughing, playing in the sun. I was a child, I was alone, I wanted to see others. So, I watched you play outside, watched you stand alone at your mother's grave, watched you juggle…"

Genevieve stared at him in surprise.

"I saw you dancing, dipping your feet in the moat, casting off the layers of clothes and corsets so you could be free. I took you because I didn't want you to jump off that balcony…I took you because…"

He heaved a deep sigh, and rested his forehead on hers. "It was wrong, but I wanted you. To know your name, feel your warmth."

He pressed himself against her and the pang of pleasure rang through her body like the vibrations of a bell. Genevieve found her arms rising, closing around his waist. His hands released their grip and pushed her sleeves down even further.

"You were all alone up here," she whispered.

"You must tell me to stop. Even now I find it hard to control myself. You become warmer each time I touch you. Tell me to stop…"

"But I don't want you to," Genevieve whispered.

He pushed her dress down. It fell to her waist.

"Tell me to stop."

"No."

"But it's not right."

"I know what it is to be alone," Genevieve said as she reached up and slipped her hand under his shirt. The prince sighed deeply at her touch and pressed his hands against her breasts. Genevieve jumped in surprise as her nipples hardened. He pressed them between his fingers, making her pang of want spread, it traveled through her stomach down between her legs. He massaged the swell of her bosom in his hands, sighing with need. Genevieve felt something press against her thigh as his erection grew.

"What is your name?" she whispered, running her hands over his chest and stomach, down to the line of his pants.

"Adrian," he whispered back, sliding his hands away

from her breasts and down the slope of her waist. He grabbed her hips and lifted her up, pressing her against the wall. He rested his face on her neck, sniffing her hair. Legs lifted, Genevieve could feel his erection pressed firmly against her nether region. "Tell me yours."

"G-Genevieve…"

"Genevieve," he pressed his bare chest to hers, shifting so that her nipples brushed over him, making her shudder with arousal. She could feel his teeth graze her neck. "I took you because I fell in love with you from far away. It's not fair and I'm sorry."

Genevieve didn't know what to say. She was overwhelmed, scared and ravenous at the same time. She wanted him to remove his pants and at the same time to stay just as he was, holding her.

"I wanted you to know who I was. I watched your happiness and your deepest sorrow. I saw you become strong and beautiful. I wanted only to know your name. If that's the only thing you wish to share with me, then please tell me to stop."

Genevieve leaned forward, pressing her lips against his ear. "Keep going."

It was all he needed. Adrian set her feet back on the ground and pushed her dress past her hips. Genevieve's fingers went to his belt and pulled it free. She undid the button there and he pushed them down, revealing his hard member.

His hands returned to her hips and picked her up again. Genevieve gasped as she felt the head of his penis press against her opening. She was surprised by how wet she was. He rubbed himself against her folds, coaxing her open. Genevieve shuddered and wrapped her arms around his neck, holding on tight as he carefully pressed himself inside her.

There was a moment of pain, quickly replaced by a much stronger sensation as he eased himself back, then in again, deeper each time. Genevieve's pang of pleasure was satisfied, only to be replaced by something deeper and stronger. She could feel him pressing against something inside her, something that sent waves of deliciousness through her whole body. She wrapped her legs around his back and buried her face in his neck. Every time he thrust into her, she wanted more.

She whimpered and moved against him eagerly, urging him to go faster. The prince complied, thrusting his pelvis with more force. Genevieve cried out in surprise.

"Are you alright?" he murmured.

"Very."

He went faster, deeper, each thrust produced a small yelp from Genevieve, who panted with effort. The sensations inside of her were overwhelming, she didn't know what to do with herself, only knew that she wanted more...more...

"More..." she gasped.

Adrian grabbed her buttocks, lifting her up and letting her fall onto his pelvis. She cried out as he did it again, and again. Each time, her body seized up, it was as if each thrust had built up inside of her, one on top of the other and suddenly imploded, leaving behind the most immense satisfaction she had ever experienced.

"Adrian…" she gasped.

"O-oh…" Adrian moaned, squeezing her cheeks in his hands, still pumping. He lowered her to the ground, resting her on his discarded cloak. He sat on all fours over her, staring down at her eyes as he neared climax.

Genevieve had never seen anything so beautiful as those ice-hard eyes melting, softening as they gazed upon her.

He lifted her legs and Genevieve cried out as another round of thrusts sent her reeling to another orgasm. She grabbed his hips, getting close.

"Don't stop," she begged.

He reached a hand down and touched her clitoris, pressing his cool fingers against it. Genevieve choked on a cry as the two sensations combined, sending her over the edge. He rolled her pearl under his finger, sending electricity through her body.

Adrian gasped and pushed himself deep inside her as he came, an expression of bliss washing over his face. Genevieve took gulps of air, trying to catch her breath. Adrian's arms trembled as he pulled out of her and lowered himself to rest his head on her stomach.

Genevieve stroked his hair as he hugged her hips.

"Genevieve…"

Chapter Five

THE WITCH WALKED THROUGH THE snow, wrapped in a cloak. In one hand she carried her hourglass—the sand was dangerously low. In her other hand she held a birdcage, inside of which a tiny Malaya laid, unconscious.

The Witch carried a wicked dagger on her waist.

She walked through the woods, following a tiny trail. There were no friendly evergreens in this part of the wood, only bare skeleton trees reaching their limbs toward a darkening sky.

The Witch entered a small clearing—almost a perfect circle cleared of trees. In the middle there was a small table covered in a lace tablecloth. Two chairs and two settings were set up, with a tea set waiting.

The witch placed the bird cage containing Malaya on the ground, and sat down. She poured some tea. She set her hourglass on the table—it was almost empty. She calmly put milk and sugar in her tea, then looked up across the table.

The sand ran out of the hourglass. A single grain hesitated in the neck, and stopped.

The witch sipped her tea, and lowered the cup.

"I've been waiting for you."

The Grim Reaper sat across from her, as if it had been there all along. It was a black cloak with nothing inside, as if an invisible person were wearing it. A scythe rested against its chair.

"Would you like some tea?"

Adrian raised his head and breathed deeply, catching a scent.

"There it is."

"What?" Genevieve looked up, halfway to putting her dress back on.

"Black magic." Adrian was already in his pants. He pulled his shirt over his head and went to the door. "The Witch has made her move. I can sense death in the air. She has summoned it."

"The Witch? She summoned—"

"She's the one behind this. I must go."

Genevieve made to follow him. He placed a hand on her shoulder.

"Stay here, please."

She grabbed his wrist and he smiled.

"You're too stubborn for you own good," he said fondly.

"What is the Witch doing? What do you mean she summoned death?"

"I'm not sure why, but she's the one who wanted the

princess, not me. I saw through her manipulation, and decided to find out what she was after."

"That's why you attacked the castle?"

"She said my future depended on it, but I believe it is *her* future she's worried about, that's why Death is here. Since I hover between living and dead I can sense it when it is near. I'm not sure what its presence means, but the dungeons are the safest place in the castle. Stay here."

He pulled away from her grip and slipped through the door.

"Prince Adrian!"

He smiled at her and shut the door. Genevieve reached for the handle, but a noise caught her attention. She turned her head toward the cell window.

A girl stood there, faded and transparent, staring at Genevieve with a blank face. She couldn't have been more than ten years old, yet her dark eyes held wisdom beyond her years. Eyes that reminded Genevieve of the Toymaker.

I can sense death in the air.

If Death itself was on the castle grounds, what did that mean for the dead?

"M'Kala?"

The girl did not speak, but she raised her hand to her lips and kissed her fingers, then offered the hand to Genevieve, blowing her a kiss.

From the cell window snow suddenly fell between the bars as a pair of legs walked past. M'Kala disappeared as the flakes cascaded right through her body.

"Wait!" Genevieve cried out in surprise, reaching for the place where the girl had been standing.

"Genevieve!"

She jumped as the Jester's face appeared in the window, her mouth dropped.

"Dad!"

She ran to the window and reached her hands through the bars. He took them and squeezed, smiling. "Are you okay? Did he hurt you?"

"No, no, I'm alright. I can't believe you came for me."

The Jester reached his hand through the bars and cupped her cheek. "Of course I did, and I'm going to get you out of there."

He produced his sword and struck it against the bars to no affect. He began sawing at one instead.

"Dad?"

He looked up. Genevieve walked across the room and opened the unlocked door.

"Well that's not a very good bloody dungeon is it?"

The Jester ran around the castle to the front door, while Genevieve ran through the halls to meet him at the front hall. Outside, the snow was falling heavily, and Genevieve tried to ignore the cold.

"This has to do with a witch then?" the Jester asked as Genevieve explained what she knew.

"We need to find out where they went. The prince may be in danger."

"Malaya as well. Something took her in the woods, and if the Witch was after her, then that's where we'll find them."

They searched the snow-covered ground, easily

finding footprints. They followed them toward the dark woods on the other side of the castle.

As they entered the trees, however, there was a crash of shrubbery, and Kyran appeared, ramming into the Jester, almost knocking him off his feet.

"Hey!" Genevieve marched forward to block him, but the Jester retaliated, somersaulting through the snow and onto his feet, drawing his sword.

"What's this then? Didn't learn your lesson the first time?"

"I am here to take the princess, but first I need to know who the better man is." Kyran pointed his sword threateningly.

"Go on, Gen. I'll be with you shortly."

Genevieve frowned, not moving.

Kyran attacked, the Jester easily parried, entering a fighting stance. Genevieve's eyes widened. "Dad?"

"Go!"

Genevieve shook her head in disbelief, turned, and ran into the woods. He could obviously take care of himself.

The Jester and Kyran fought hard. The Jester performed acrobatics with his sword play, back flipping and dodging Kyran's blows.

"Who taught you how to sword fight, a blind man?" the Jester taunted.

Kyran charged him in a rage. The Jester caught his sword at the hilt and flipped it out of his hand. He began to juggle the two swords teasingly.

"I mean, come on, I'm a jester and you can't even beat me?"

"You are no jester," Kyran spat.

"Really? I must look very silly wearing this jingly hat then."

"Who are you? Tell me!"

The Jester's expression suddenly became hard and serious. He pointed both swords at Kyran's neck, forcing him to his knees.

"Oh, no, no, I want this. I want the rumors to follow you home, back to your kingdom. I want everyone to know that the great Prince Kyran was beaten by Malaya's fool. You thought you could take the poor girl like she was something to be owned, and I want you to go back with nothing, not even your dignity. If I see you again, I'll take the last valuable thing you have...your life."

The Jester turned and threw Kyran's sword. It spun through the air, the blade embedding itself into the trunk of a tree.

"Do you understand?"

Kyran glared, but nodded stiffly.

"Then go."

Kyran stood, shoulders sagging in defeat, and walked away. The Jester turned his gaze to the woods, griped his sword tightly, and marched forward.

"Good to see you again," the Witch said, setting her cup in its saucer. The Grim Reaper put a cube of sugar into his tea. "I know that you probably hear this from everyone, wanting more time, but not everyone can actually meet you like a witch can."

The Grim Reaper continued to put sugar cubes in its tea, unanswering.

"I want to make a deal with you. One soul for another."

It reached for another cube, but its sleeve met an empty bowl. It sagged in defeat.

"And not just any soul," the Witch continued. She picked up the bird cage and set it on the table. She opened the door and dragged Malaya's unconscious body out onto the table. "The soul of a princess."

Genevieve ran down the trail as fast as she could. Her bare feet ached from the cold and her body grew numb. When she reached the end of the trail she almost crashed into the Frozen Prince. He looked down at her and put a finger to his lips.

Genevieve looked around him and saw the Witch, sitting at a table. Then she saw Malaya.

Genevieve started to charge forward, but the prince grabbed her shoulder and leaned down to whisper in her ear.

"I need you to be careful in this. I will approach them, but the passing of a witch is unsafe, and death has a strange presence here. For now, just watch, use your instinct."

It was only then that Genevieve realized there was a second figure at the table, one that was very much not human. She gasped and stepped back, bumping into Adrian's chest.

"I-I don't know how..."

"You told me you knew who you were."

"Why did you ask me?"

"I have known you for only a few hours and in that time, I have seen you as a warrior, and a child. And now, I need you to be who you are."

The prince straightened, and entered the clearing.

"Do we have a deal?" the Witch asked, holding out her hand to shake.

The prince's hand clasped her wrist. "Enough."

The Witch snapped her head around, glaring at him.

"You're too late!" She stood up, knocking her chair over and pulling the dagger from her belt. She raised it to stab Malaya, lying unconscious on the table. The prince acted quickly, snatching the tiny princess as the dagger came down, the blade meeting table instead.

The prince backed away, cuddling Malaya to his chest.

"Is this really your wish? She's an innocent girl."

The Witch's hair began to rise, and her fingernails grew into claws. "She wouldn't be the first."

Genevieve's eyes widened in understanding, and she stepped into the clearing. "You killed M'kala!"

The witch's head snapped around, glaring at her.

"That's why she's still here. You've done this before! You made a deal with Death—"

"That's right, and once a deal is made there's no going back."

"Until someone dies," Adrian said.

The Grim Reaper sat in its chair and sipped its tea.

Adrian narrowed his eyes. Ice formed at his feet, a snowy wind whipped around his body. The witch raised her arms to the sky and snapped her fingers. A ring of fire suddenly burst around the circle, trapping them inside.

Outside the clearing, the Jester scrambled to a stop, almost running into the wall of flame. He looked around desperately, and began to climb a tree.

"I warned you a fire was coming," the Witch said. She charged at him, swiping her claws at his face. The prince winced and stumbled back. The Witch clasped his wrists, trying to get to Malaya.

Adrian dropped Malaya, pushing the Witch back. Her claws raked his chest, tearing his shirt open.

Genevieve sprinted forward, falling over Malaya and shielding her with her body. The Witch broke free of Adrian and slashed at Genevieve's back. Long claw marks appeared in a burst of red. Genevieve screamed in pain.

The prince's eyes flashed in anger. He seized the Witch by the neck and swung her around, holding her in the air. The Witch struggled to breathe.

"What will you do, my prince? Kill me?"

The prince didn't answer, but slowly lowered her down.

"You know no one leaves this circle until someone dies."

The prince turned away and looked at Genevieve who struggled to her knees. The Witch's eyes widened.

"No! Don't you dare!"

The prince dropped her. She went to her knees, gasping for air. The prince advanced on Genevieve, snow billowing around him, frost covering the ground with each step.

The Witch crawled across the ground toward the fallen dagger.

The prince bowed and cupped Genevieve's face in his cold hands. Genevieve shook her head, realizing what he meant to do.

The Witch rose and threw the dagger at Genevieve. The girl screamed as the blade pierced her shoulder. Adrian spun and bared his teeth at the old woman.

"You can't do this! I won't let you die!" the Witch screamed.

Adrian turned back to Genevieve, taking her in his arms. He quickly pulled the dagger out, making her wince. Genevieve panted in pain, blood flowing, staining the snow. Adrian touched her shoulder, sealing wound with ice.

"Stop! Don't kiss him!"

The Grim Reaper stood and walked toward them.

The Frozen Prince smiled and leaned forward to kiss her.

The Witch stood, blocking the Grim Reaper's path. "Don't take him, I didn't want this."

The Grim Reaper seemed to stare at her, not moving. Confused, the Witch looked down, realizing that something was wrong.

A sword stuck out of her chest.

Behind her, the Jester sat in a tree, looking over the wall of fire, hand still posed from his throw.

On the table, the last grain of sand fell through the hourglass, and the Witch fell with it.

The prince pressed his lips to Genevieve's tenderly.

"I thought...you didn't believe...in fairy tales," she whispered when the kiss ended. Blood blossomed across his shirt where his old wound lay. He smiled and kissed her forehead. Genevieve closed her eyes, passing out.

The fire slowly died. The heavily falling snow covered the clearing, muffling all sound. The Jester walked into the clearing and bowed deeply.

"Your majesty."

"It's good to see you again, Nathaniel," Adrian said.

The Jester smiled. "I wasn't sure if you would recognize me."

"I didn't, I recognized your sword throw. The only knight who has ever mastered such a move." The prince rose, picking Genevieve up in his arms. "I never got to thank you for trying to save me that night, you are a worthy knight."

The Jester bowed his head. Adrian passed Genevieve to him. "Take her, quickly."

There was a small moan behind them. They turned to see Malaya, grown back to her normal size, waking up. The Jester went to her side.

"My lady? If you can stand, please do, we must go."

The Frozen Prince walked away from them and took a seat at the table, hand moving to his chest in pain.

Malaya looked around uncertainly, but stood up.

"I'll explain everything. Come on."

The Jester guided the two girls away, but hesitated at the edge of the clearing. "My prince, is there anything—"

"Just take care of her. Everything is written out to you. Take the carriage."

The Jester stared at him with sadness, bowed his head, and walked away.

The Frozen Prince looked down at his chest, his wound was bleeding profusely now. He looked up across the table, where the Grim Reaper had taken a seat once again, watching, and waiting. He looked at the bright red on his hand curiously. He leaned back in his chair and closed his eyes.

The snow stopped falling.

Chapter Six

GENEVIEVE OPENED HER EYES, remembered what happened, and sat up.

She was lying in bed with the Jester sitting at her side. He smiled.

"How're you feeling?"

Genevieve didn't answer. "Where are we?" she asked instead.

"I borrowed the prince's carriage and took us to the nearest village. We're at an inn at the bottom of the mountain. A doctor took care of you last night, gave you a sedative so that you would remain asleep. I sent word to Malaya's parents, they'll be arriving soon."

"Where is Malaya?"

"She's fine. She stayed with you all night. Now it's her turn to sleep."

"And Prince Adrian..." but the expression on the Jester's face told the tale. Genevieve sagged back into bed. Her shoulder and back hurt from her wounds, but both were surpassed by the breaking of her heart.

"Our kiss broke the curse."

"I'm sorry, my love. I tried to save him, but I think this was what he wanted."

"What do you mean?"

"He saw me ready to throw my sword at the Witch, but he kissed you anyway."

Genevieve sniffed and wiped her eyes, but new tears quickly replaced those. She settled for crying into her pillow. The Jester rubbed her back.

"He was a dear friend of mine. When he was a boy I was his personal guard, a loyal servant and friend. He was a kind prince, unspoiled. I loved him very much."

Genevieve looked up in surprise. "You knew him? You were a knight?"

"More than a knight, I was a nobleman. After the castle was attacked I had to go into hiding. The rebels were looking for any member of the royal family, killing anyone who might rise up to reclaim the throne, and though my relationship was distant and not by blood, I couldn't risk it. I joined a traveling theater, then was taken on as a court jester. I think that's why Hanna wanted to keep you a secret. She couldn't risk anyone finding out who you were."

"Who am I?" Genevieve whispered.

"Besides me, you are the last member of our royal family. By all rights you are the heir to the throne, and with the passing of the Frozen Prince, that throne does fall to you, Princess Genevieve."

Genevieve shook her head, leaning back and pressing

her palms against her eyes as fresh tears fell. The Jester took her hands and squeezed them.

"No, that's...I'm just a laundry girl. The daughter of a washerwoman and a jester."

Her father smiled. "Funny how that worked out, huh?"

Genevieve stayed in bed while her father left to search for food. She stared out the window while her heart ached and her mind whirled with the miraculous information she had just received.

Princess Genevieve.

She shook her head. It was too absurd. How could she claim the throne of a man she only got to love for a day? How could she live in his castle without his ghost haunting her? Fresh tears threatened to form when a knock came at her door.

"Enter," she said, struggling to repress the hitch in her voice.

The door opened and Malaya came in. Genevieve was surprised to see her in pants and riding boots. She rose and opened her arms and the two fell into an embrace, sobbing openly.

"I can't believe you came for me."

"Oh, Gen, I would never leave you. Not after what you did for me."

They held each other for a long while until they were finally able to stop crying, telling each other how proud they were of one another, and how happy it made them to have each other back.

"Gen, I hope you'll forgive me," Malaya said, squeezing her hands, "but I have to return to the mountain before my parents arrive."

"But why?"

Malaya lowered her head, and Genevieve saw her cheeks glow pink. "There was a man we met. He helped us get up the mountain to find you. When the guards found us, he led them away and…I have to find him, make sure he's alright, and thank him."

"A mountain man? Whoever is he?"

"That's the thing…oh, you'll think me so silly. *I* feel silly, falling for a thief."

"No!"

"He's the Bandit of the Northern Mountain."

Genevieve couldn't help it, she grinned.

"Don't make fun of me! It's bad, Gen, father will never forgive me."

"I hope this isn't a girlish fling," Genevieve said seriously.

"Perhaps it is. Maybe I was just swept up by the adventure and his rebellious nature. I just…he didn't treat me like a princess, or, rather, he did, but he never acted like I owed him anything because I was a woman. He seemed happy with the idea of earning my affection."

Genevieve smiled with understanding. "You really like him, don't you?"

The blush deepened.

"Then we must go." Genevieve hopped out of bed and started searching for clothes.

"Are you sure, Gen? You're still injured."

"I'm very sure. We must find this man and, as you say, properly thank him."

Anything was better than lying in bed, hurting. At least this way she wouldn't have to think about Adrian or her new title.

"There are some clothes in my room," Malaya said, "I had the inn keeper send them to me. Go change, I'll pen a note for your father."

Genevieve nodded and went to Malaya's room. On the bed was a variety of clothes the inn keeper had sent up. Most appeared to be hand-me-downs, most likely from one of the inn keeper's own children. Genevieve followed Malaya's example and selected pants and boots for the journey.

The girls met in the hall and snuck out the back through the kitchen, avoiding the Jester. At the inn's stable, Malaya tossed her name about until they were given two horses with the promise of paying later. They mounted and rode back toward the mountain.

It didn't take long for Genevieve to regret her decision to join Malaya. Her back hurt from her injuries and the rest of her body was sore as well from the mistreatment of the past two days.

Had it really just been two days? It seemed a whole lifetime had passed. Genevieve punched her thigh, casting the thoughts away. She had to focus on helping Malaya, not her own troubles.

"So, what happened to you once you were parted from this bandit?" Genevieve asked.

"It's hard to recall," Malaya said, "I know I was

attacked by something – some sort of shadowy creature that transported me into the Witch's lair. I was so disoriented that she was able to force a liquid down my throat. I don't know what it did to me, but I could feel my body going through turmoil and I passed out. When I woke we were outside. Your dad told me what happened while you were unconscious.

"We found the prince's carriage, and this other man came out of the castle. He helped us hitch up the horse, but I never learned who he was."

Genevieve stiffened. The Toymaker, of course, she had completely forgotten. Would he still be at the castle? She hoped so, she wanted to make sure he was alright.

"This place seems different," Malaya commented. They had been riding for a while, and were well into the mountain wilderness now. Genevieve studied their surroundings.

"I wasn't fully aware when I first passed through here," she said, "what's different?"

"Something…just seems off."

Genevieve studied the landscape around them, the steep, rocky terrain was filled with trees and some low brush. Despite the full sun there seemed to be a deepness to the shadows. Genevieve then noticed the absence of the sounds of birds and insects.

"You're right," she said softly.

A dead witch, a broken curse…what else did this mountain contain?

They urged the horses to go a little faster, continuing down the trail. The animals seemed restless, however, reluctant and slow. Malaya and Genevieve exchanged nervous glances.

"What's that sound?" Malaya gasped.

It was a thundering sound, like a stampede, growing louder. Suddenly, animals came running through the brush: squirrels, rabbits, foxes, all sorts of creatures ran past them. The horses squealed and reared up, trying to buck off their riders. Genevieve fell, hitting the ground hard, and Malaya quickly jumped off her horse. The horses retreated with the rest of the animals.

Genevieve winced in pain. The pain from her shoulder wound flared and she remained on the ground while animals ran past her. Malaya went to her side.

They heard a panicked cry from a rabbit, and looked up to see two wolves had also joined the fray. Seeing the girls, however, the wolves froze, ears flattened in suspicion. Malaya stood protectively in front of Genevieve, grabbing a stick. The wolves growled in response.

"What's wrong with them?" Malaya hissed. Genevieve saw it too—a strange blackness in their eyes, a foul smell from their mouths. Malaya swung her stick at them, screaming. The wolves growled and snarled. One decided to attack, and Malaya slammed the stick across its nose.

Genevieve struggled to her feet and grabbed a rock. She threw it at the second wolf, hitting it with enough force that it reconsidered providing backup to its partner.

There was a shout from the trees and a man came charging forward, brandishing a fiery torch. Startled, the wolves retreated from the flames, following the rest of the animals down the mountain.

Genevieve beamed. "You're okay!"

The Toymaker turned and smiled at them in turn. "I don't know what you're doing back on this mountain, but I'm glad I found you."

Genevieve ran forward and hugged him tightly. "What's happening?"

"That's a long story, but first, I have a message for you. I was actually coming down the mountain, hoping to catch you."

"What is it?"

He looked into her eyes, twinkling as he smiled. "He's alive."

It was as if her very blood ceased to flow. "What?"

"The prince is alive," he took her hand and stroked it with his fingers, "I'm telling you the truth. After you left I found him in the woods. Cold bastard tried to bleed out on me."

"You...you saved him?"

"I told you, I can fix absolutely anything. Even broken hearts." He squeezed her hand tightly.

Tears began to fall. She felt Malaya's arms around her, and then the Toymaker's. "We have to go. I must see him."

"I'm afraid it's not so simple," the Toymaker warned. "As I said, it's a long story, but you've seen for yourself that the mountain is dangerous. We need to leave and I will tell you all."

"I'm not leaving without Roland," Malaya said firmly.

"Who?"

"A man she met on the mountain," Genevieve said, "he helped her and my father reach the castle."

"Where is he?"

"In the abandoned village," Malaya said.

"That's not far, and I know the safe routes. We'll go there and I'll explain what has happened."

The Toymaker motioned for them to follow and they continued through the forest's darkening trails. Genevieve looked up toward the mountain top where the prince's castle was located.

Alive.

He was alive.

But what was the dark force encompassing the mountain? Genevieve shivered. Malaya took her arm, smiling reassuringly. They stayed close together, following the Toymaker, who led them down ancient roads and overgrown trails, his torch lighting the way.

Adrian woke to pain and darkness. He struggled to see, but colors and light blurred. Was he dead?

No, but you'll wish you were...

Adrian stiffened. That voice...he hadn't heard that voice since the night his heart was frozen.

You broke my curse, little prince, I didn't think you could find someone who could look past your icy heart. Unfortunately, for you, it has melted my prison as well.

"You're the one...from that night."

Yes.

"The one who placed the curse on me." Adrian

struggled to rise, but something bound his arms against his sides.

A curse you asked for. Do not make me the villain in this. You wanted the strength to avenge your family, you wanted to live, I gave what was in my power to give.

Adrian winced as he felt himself lifted, arms pinned by a foreign body that snaked up around him. His chest hurt. He felt hot.

"What do you want?"

I want the power that is owed to me. When your family claimed this land my own influence was smothered and I was pushed away beneath the mountain. They used to worship me here, slaughter animals and spill their blood for me. So, when the blood of my oppressors fell, it was a sacrifice to my own power, and I rose.

Adrian's eyesight started to clear, and he could make out the creature that held him captive. A large brown thing, twisted and sharp with the bones that lay flushed against its skin, long fingers like grasping tree branches, eyes like the void.

I thought my curse would give me control, but alas...you were too strong.

"Still am," Adrian spat.

But there is another, the creature said, *one of royal blood, who has returned to my mountain. Your death would be an excellent sacrifice for my return, but for now...*

Adrian gritted his teeth as the coils of the creature's tail tightened around him.

...I have a different use for you.

• • •

The Jester read the letter Malaya had left for him, explaining that they would be back before dark, that she only wanted to make sure Roland was alright, that Genevieve was with her.

He groaned and clutched his hair in frustration. He had just gotten his daughter off the mountain and now she was climbing back up. Well, he wasn't going after her. The danger was over, they could get back on their own.

"I'm not going after them," the Jester said to himself, crossing his arms, "they're fine. I'm not climbing up that bloody mountain again."

The Jester heard the sound of horse hooves and wheels on cobblestone. Looking out the window, he saw the royal carriage approaching, with a very angry looking king sitting inside.

"You know what? I'm going after them."

The Jester didn't bother to pack or get a horse. He left through the back door and ran.

Chapter Seven

MALAYA GAVE A CRY OF recognition as they came upon the abandoned village. "This is the one! This is where the bandits live!"

"I wondered who had been robbing our caravans," the Toymaker muttered. Malaya took the lead, jogging through the streets to the inn. Genevieve followed more slowly, studying the dark, empty buildings they passed. The glass windows were cracked and covered in dust. Vines grew over walls while tree roots tilled the cobblestones of the road. She felt watched and uneasy, as if something were gazing at her from the shadows. She remembered the wolves and their possessed eyes.

She took the Toymaker's arm. "What is happening to the mountain? Where is Prince Adrian?"

He touched her arm in turn. "I'm...not sure. But he is alive."

"Is he safe?"

The Toymaker lowered his gaze in answer.

Malaya jogged well ahead of them, reaching the inn. When she tried the door, she found it locked.

"Hello?" she called, backing away to search for any signs of life. Her answer was a call from a bird of prey. Had they left already? How would she ever find him now?

She turned back to the others. "I can't find anyone. Should we—" she was cut off by another cry from the bird, this one much louder and closer. Malaya looked up and saw a hawk swooping down toward her.

Malaya screamed and ducked, hitting the ground and covering her head. The Toymaker and Genevieve ran toward her, but the bird turned, talons out, and went for them instead. The Toymaker swung his torch at the hawk and it veered away.

"What is going on with these animals!?" Genevieve gasped, ducking low to avoid the hawk's attack. She felt its claws brush the top of her head, pulling out strands of hair.

The hawk dove toward Malaya again. The princess screamed and covered her face, pressing herself flat to the ground. She waited for the pain of the hawk's talons, but instead she felt a heavy weight fall on her, and heard the exclamation of a man's voice.

Malaya opened her eyes and turned her head to look over her shoulder. Roland's face stared down at her, his teasing grin filled her vision. His comforting weight was lifted as he jumped up and turned to face their feathered assailant. He removed a bow from his back and pulled an arrow from his quiver.

Malaya watched as he took aim, carefully following the bird as it flew toward the trees. She found her eyes wandering down his back, his shoulder was cut and bleeding where the hawk's talons had struck him. He released the arrow from the bow, and it pierced the hawk's chest, dropping it to the ground.

With a proud grin, Roland turned back to Malaya and offered his hand. She took it and he pulled her to her feet. She held on to his hand.

"You're alright."

"Of course. You weren't worried, were you?"

Malaya only smiled.

"Is this the gentleman you spoke of?" Genevieve asked, approaching them.

"Yes, this is Roland. The Bandit of the North. How did you escape the knights?"

"I wish I could give you a daring story of my stealth, but they weren't actually knights. They were just armor controlled by magic. As I ran they eventually fell apart. When I made it back to the castle you were already gone."

"I'm back now."

"Yes, indeed you are," he smirked, "let's get indoors. The animals of the mountain have been behaving strangely."

"So we noticed," Genevieve said, "do you know why?"

"No idea, unless the Thing Beneath the Mountain is back."

"What?"

"It's a childhood ghost story. I'm only joking." Roland guided them to the inn, using a key to unlock the door. He locked it again once they were all inside.

"But what is it? I've never heard such a story," Genevieve said.

"The Thing Beneath the Mountain is an ancient spirit," the Toymaker said thoughtfully, "and now that you mention it . . . it might have more merit than you think."

"How so?" Genevieve asked.

They followed Roland into the lobby and took seats around the fireplace. Roland tried to load it with wood, but winced as he used his injured shoulder. Malaya took his arm.

"Let's see to your injury first," she said.

Roland nodded in agreement. "The kitchen is just through here."

The two of them left through a side door. The Toymaker loaded the wood himself and started a fire. Genevieve scooted closer, not realizing how chilled she had become.

"What's the Thing Beneath the Mountain?" she asked.

"It had a real name one time. It was worshiped by ancient people until new cultures took over and new religions took hold. Whenever something bad happened they blamed it on the old spirit. It could control animals and influence the weather. If you went into the woods alone, the Thing Beneath the Mountain would take you. There were plenty of legends in the village."

"You think this spirit is the reason the mountain feels so...wrong?"

"I don't know, but when that bandit mentioned it, it

made me think. Something the prince said when I found him..."

The Toymaker walked through the snow and the now quiet forest. The Jester had taken the two girls and left, pointing him to where the prince remained.

He found the prince lying in the snow, bleeding from the wound he had sustained all those years ago. The Toymaker stopped the bleeding as well as he could and carried the prince back to the castle.

Inside, he tried to sew up the wound with trembling hands. A human being was much different than a wooden doll, but the same intuition that helped him to build so many beautiful toys seemed to guide his hand here as well. He sewed and patched the wound. He mopped the prince's brow, trying to hold off any fever.

"I've tried, your highness. An infection may yet still take you, but I've tried my best."

"The ice...the ice is melting..." the prince murmured, half unconscious.

"Don't try to speak, you need to rest."

"It'll get out..."

The toymaker frowned. "What will get out?"

"The creature in the mountain...don't...let it out..."

He passed out, breathing haggardly. The Toymaker shuddered, clutching his hand. He had to get the prince to a proper doctor.

The Toymaker went to the stables. The carriage had been taken. All they had left was the wagon for carrying supplies. It would have to do. He hitched up a horse and loaded the wagon with blankets, trying to make is as comfortable as he could.

He managed to wake the prince long enough to get him into the wagon, but even that short journey left Adrian flushed and sweating, and he immediately lost consciousness. The Toymaker bundled him up and took the reins, urging the horse forward as quickly as he dared.

He could feel a stillness in the woods, a deepening of shadows as they rode. The horse seemed nervous and the Toymaker worried. He lit one of the wagon torches with a match, trying to find comfort in the light.

He saw animal eyes staring at him from the trees and the bushes, but heard no sounds. The horse was galloping now, he couldn't get it to slow, no matter how hard he pulled on the reins. The wagon teetered dangerously, threatening to crash as they took a sharp turn.

Then the horse suddenly stopped. The Toymaker was almost thrown off the wagon, but managed to hang on to his seat. The forest seemed darker now, even though it was day. The horse remained frozen in place.

The Toymaker raised his torch and saw a face staring down at him. He screamed and fell back into the wagon bench. The monster stood as tall as a house, with starved, lanky limbs, hollow eyes, and a tangle of strange fur.

It reached its arm forward, over the Toymaker, and picked up the prince in its long fingers. The Toymaker protested, yelling and waving his torch at the creature, but it paid him no mind. It clutched the prince to its chest and backed away, disappearing into the shadows until only its glowing eyes remained.

The Toymaker jumped off the wagon and tried to chase it down, but then even the eyes were gone, and he was alone.

"I continued to search the woods for the prince. I was about to return to the castle when I heard you and the princess, and saw the wolves attacking you."

Genevieve hugged herself, trying not to tremble. "Where could it have taken him? We have to get him back. What *is* it?"

"I don't know."

"Does it have something to do with his curse? We only heard of it when the curse was broken."

"Possibly. For now, I will be returning to the castle and see if I can track his whereabouts. I would ask you to return home, but I have a feeling that order will go unheeded."

"Good instinct," Genevieve said, "there's no chance I'm leaving him to that monster."

"Then rest up. Once the others are ready we'll leave."

Malaya pulled Roland's shirt down, cleaning the gash on his shoulder. It wasn't deep, so she cleaned the blood and bound it with fabric until the bleeding stopped. The kitchen was equipped with a water pump and plenty of clean cloth to use.

"So, you came back to the mountain to find me," Roland said casually, looking at her over his shoulder as she worked. "What should I take this as a sign of?"

"Only that I owed you a debt for helping us and I wanted to make sure you were alright."

"So why not send someone else? Princesses shouldn't be hiking through woods by themselves."

"Well...perhaps I wanted to see you."

"Oh?"

Malaya cleared her throat, using all the tricks her tutor had taught her to appear that she was in charge, that she wasn't nervous. She secured his bandages. Roland unbuttoned his shirt and tossed it aside.

He reached forward and touched her cheek with the tips of his fingers. "You're cute when you blush."

Malaya straightened out of his reach. "I'm not blushing, just winded from the trip."

"I'm glad you wanted to see me again. I wanted to see you too."

Malaya smiled.

Roland leaned forward and took her face in his hands. When she didn't pull away he pressed his lips against hers, filling her with the scent of tobacco and wood. Malaya inhaled deeply and leaned into him, her hands coming up to his bare chest. Her heart hammered at the very idea of touching a man like this.

Roland's hands touched her as well, moving from her cheeks, to her shoulders, to her chest.

Malaya gasped and jumped away.

"Now you are *definitely* blushing." He said with a teasing laugh.

"I—we should..."

"No, no, it's not time to leave yet. Please. I may never see you again after this. Please, don't leave..."

Malaya's lips parted in surprise. Roland's joking demeanor disappeared as he wrapped her in his arms. His eyes begging, his touch searching. He kissed her face, then her neck.

"I can't lie with you, Roland," Malaya said, wincing at her own words.

"I don't need to remove my pants to pleasure you, my lady," Roland whispered into her ear, tongue flicking against her lobe. Malaya felt goosebumps cascade down her body, it was as if the goosebumps were inside her.

"Please, let me just...let's just have this moment."

Malaya nodded.

Roland lifted her up and sat her on the table, continuing his kisses. Each kiss sent a jolt between her legs, she felt herself becoming wet. Roland took her shirt and pulled it off.

Malaya turned her head and tried to cover herself, but Roland grabbed her wrists and forced her arms away from her chest.

"God, you are beautiful," he breathed, staring at her. Malaya trembled.

His lips traveled over her collarbone, down to her breasts. He cupped one in his hand, massaging it with his fingers. Malaya sighed as a euphoric feeling washed over her, dampening her trepidation. She wrapped her arms around his neck as he buried his face in her mounds, kissing, and licking, and sighing deliciously.

He crawled up onto the table, pushing her back. He straightened up, looking down at her.

"I like you here, between my legs."

Malaya blushed and tried to cover herself again. Roland grinned and grabbed her pants, yanking them down in one go. Malaya gasped and tried to back away, but he grabbed her legs and pulled her back.

"Where do you think you're going?"

Malaya looked away. Her arousal was sending confusing thoughts through her head. She wanted him, badly, but she was a princess. She had been warned so many times about men.

"Trust me," Roland whispered, rubbing her thigh comfortingly. "I'll stop whenever you want me to, but give me a chance first."

She nodded.

Roland leaned down and kissed her stomach. Malaya smiled and opted to enjoy the sensation, running her hands over his muscular arms as he continued to kiss her and squeeze her breasts.

Slowly his kisses went lower and lower. He gently bit her hips, making her giggle, and ran his tongue over her thighs. Then his tongue went to her folds. Malaya stiffened.

"Shh," Roland whispered, pressing his mouth against her womanhood. Malaya melted, feeling his tongue press against her clitoris, making her wet. She felt his tongue go inside her and she gasped.

She looked down at him. He looked up at her. Malaya was burning red. Roland only hummed and continued his motions, slipping his tongue in and out of her, pressing her pearl with his fingers. It wasn't intense, but soft and relaxing. Malaya laid back and closed her eyes, smiling at the warm sensation that was building up inside of her.

She felt a jolt of arousal as he put his lips around her clitoris and sucked. She gave a soft gasp, Roland continued, pulling her into his mouth. Malaya wished she could lay her whole body against his tongue, have him lap her up.

Malaya began to pant. Roland left his mouth on her clit and put his fingers against her vagina. Malaya gasped as she felt his finger go up inside her, touching and searching as he sucked.

His finger hit a spot that made her yelp and he paused. He started to move in a rhythm, sucking her clit while his finger pressed against her moist walls. Malaya made a sound with each press, growing louder as he went faster. Malaya clutched the sides of the table, feeling overwhelmed, like something was going to pop inside of her.

Then she realized this was exactly what she wanted. The faster Roland went the more she wanted it, craved it. She moaned and leaned down into him, encouraging him to keep going. Roland complied, and she felt a second finger enter her.

Whatever was building up inside of her was only getting bigger, more urgent. Malaya moaned with need and Roland pressed himself in deeper. At last Malaya felt the release, like a cork popping off a bottle. She released one long moan and sank back against the table.

Roland removed his fingers and pressed his lips against her folds, licking her gently. Malaya could feel her vagina pulsing like a heartbeat.

"Oh, I love that feeling," Roland whispered, "I love feeling you come against me."

Malaya couldn't answer. She felt dizzy and wonderful. The world seemed brighter and her breathing was deep and steady. Roland pulled himself onto all fours over her and lowered himself down to hug her close. She could feel his erection through his pants. She tentatively reached down and touched him through the fabric, curious.

"You don't have to do anything about that," he said, nuzzling her neck.

"But, don't you need to…you know…"

"Want to? Yes, very much. Need is different."

"I want to see," Malaya said shyly.

Roland lifted himself up to his knees, raising an eyebrow at her. He unbuckled his pants. Malaya watched as he pulled his erect member from his undergarments. He palmed his balls and began to pump himself, staring down at her.

Malaya blushed and wiggled a bit, unsure of what to do. Roland grabbed her waist and pulled her hips between his knees. He continued working himself. Malaya reached forward and stroked his thigh.

Roland sighed, pumping faster. "Touch yourself."

Malaya hesitated, then cupped her breasts in her hands, pushing them up and squeezing them so that they bulged in her grip.

"Oh, yes…oh, I'm going to come…"

Malaya watched a tense bliss cross Roland's face as his hand slowed, and cum fell down onto her stomach and breasts. She gasped in surprise.

Roland sighed and sat back, sitting between her shins. He watched her as he caught his breath. "Are you alright?"

She nodded.

"I'm sorry if...if that wasn't appropriate, I just...you're so beautiful, I wanted to..." He shook his head and looked away.

Malaya smiled and touched his hand. "I liked it."

He smiled back and hopped off the table. "Let me get you a towel."

He cleaned her then held her on the table, stroking her hair and rubbing her stomach until she was relaxed and at ease.

"You're sure that was alright?" he said.

"Very much so," Malaya whispered. Her head was swimming.

"I'm glad. I don't want to hurt you in any way."

"Thank you for being so gentle with me."

Roland nodded and pressed his nose against her hair. He sighed, his brow was wrinkled with worry.

"What's wrong?"

"Nothing. We'd better get back to the others. They'll be suspicious."

"Oh no, you're right. Go find a fresh shirt, I'll get dressed."

Roland smiled at her, touching her cheek again, then turned and left the kitchen. Malaya watched him go, heart pounding.

• • •

"Gen..."

Genevieve looked up from her thoughts, seeing Malaya return from the kitchen. She had been staring at the flames of the fire, thinking of the Toymaker's tale, and had lost track of time. The Toymaker was across the room, gazing out the window. Genevieve looked up at Malaya's flushed face.

"Are you okay?" Genevieve asked

"Yes, I'm alright, but I wanted to ask you something."

Genevieve waited. Malaya saw a strange look in her eye and frowned.

"Genevieve, what's wrong?"

"The Frozen Prince is in danger," Genevieve said quietly, "I want to help him, but I don't know how."

Malaya knelt down, sitting next to her friend. "Are you going to go to the castle?"

Genevieve nodded.

"Gen, you know you don't have to," Malaya said carefully, "I know that's not really in your nature, but maybe you should just go back to your father and get back to your life."

"I love him, Malaya."

The princess's mouth dropped. "Gen..."

"I broke his curse. He...he loves me too. I know he kidnapped me, but after what we went through...I wish I could explain it. He treats me like I never thought I deserved to be treated. Desirable, powerful, beautiful."

Malaya's eyes wandered up to the stairs where Roland

was returning, dressed in a fresh shirt. "I think I understand."

Genevieve leaned her head on Malaya's shoulder. Malaya squeezed her hand. "I'll help you."

Genevieve smirked. "I think *you're* the one who needs to go back home."

"What about Roland? What if he and his bandits help us?"

"Help with what?" Roland asked, approaching them.

"Going to the castle," Genevieve answered.

"Most of my men ran once the animals started turning on us. I stayed only because I have nowhere else to go. I can guide you, but it's dangerous."

"Too dangerous to return," the Toymaker agreed, rejoining them. "I'm afraid there's not much we can do for the prince at this point."

"I have to try," Genevieve said.

The Toymaker opened his arms, showing his empty palms. "With what?"

Genevieve suddenly perked up, the answer coming to her in a heartbeat. "The Witch...she had a lair in the castle. If we can get in, maybe we could find something to use against this creature."

Everyone exchanged looks, weighing the options in their minds.

"We don't know anything about witchcraft," Malaya said, "how will we find what we need?"

"I'll go through the books, surely I'll find something."

Roland shrugged. "I'll take you if you're determined."

"Quite," Genevieve said, nodding.

"Me too," Malaya said.

"My dear friend," Genevieve took Malaya's hands and smiled at her gently, "you have done so much for me, I can't ask you to do this too. Your parents are coming, you can't break their hearts again."

"But, Gen, I can't leave you alone." Malaya looked up at Roland, but he only smiled. Malaya saw pain in his expression. "I'm not ready for this to be over. I've never been so free."

"We can't stay on the mountain," Genevieve said, patting her hand, "you have other work to do."

"What is that?"

"Convincing your father to send help, and telling my father that I'm okay."

Malaya laughed. "I can't convince father of anything."

"I have a feeling you'll be able to now."

Malaya nodded, remembering how good it felt to fight back, to be in charge. "You're right. I'll get reinforcements, and this time I won't fail."

"I'll go with you, princess," the Toymaker said.

Genevieve nodded. "No time to lose then."

Malaya and Genevieve exchanged a tight hug.

"Be careful," Malaya ordered.

"I'm proud of you, you know."

"And I of you."

They parted and the group split. The Toymaker and Malaya headed back down the mountain, while Roland readied his bow and guided Genevieve to the road that would take them to the castle.

"You keep looking over your shoulder," the Toymaker noted.

"I just..." Malaya stared at her friends' retreating backs.

"You know what you need to do to help them."

Malaya pursed her lips and nodded determinedly. She turned and didn't look back again.

"Malaya was going to tell me something," Genevieve remembered aloud. She and Roland had been walking quietly, alert for any animal attacks.

"Hm?" Roland walked a step ahead, turning his head to and fro, watching the shadows.

"What do you suppose it could have been?"

He didn't answer.

"She cares for you. It was her idea to return to the wilderness and find you."

Roland sighed. "It's an ill-fated relationship."

"So, you like her too?"

"Very much, but it doesn't change the fact that it wouldn't work. I was glad you sent her away."

Genevieve hesitated, then said, "Don't give up on her just yet."

"I think it would be better for her if I did."

"It would be better for her reputation and her family, but not for her. Don't push her away just because it seems like the right thing to do."

"Isn't it?" Roland slowed so that they were walking side by side.

"I know another couple who turned away from each

other because circumstances became difficult. It seemed like the right thing to do, but...it wasn't. Love is the right thing to do."

Roland considered her words, growing quiet again.

"I'm not saying it'll work. Only to give it a chance."

They could feel eyes watching them, but nothing attacked them, and the higher they climbed, the quieter things became.

Finally, the towers of the castle appeared and Genevieve quickened her pace.

"Easy, lass," Roland warned, "we need a way in that won't draw attention."

"But I don't see anything."

"Me neither. Makes you worry, right? Come on, let's try the servants' entrance."

They circled around the castle, staying hidden in the trees. As they neared the back, a growl sent them jumping out of the shadows. Roland spun and fired his arrow. The point barely struck its target—a bear that came barreling out of the brush.

Genevieve screamed as Roland was knocked over and trampled. The bear came at her. She ran, seeing the same emptiness in its eyes that she had seen in the wolves' eyes. She waited for its teeth or claws to catch her, but it did not. She risked a glance over her shoulder, and while the bear pursued her, it didn't seem to be hunting her, but rather *herding* her.

Genevieve caught one last glance at Roland, who was weakly rolling over and reaching for his bow. Genevieve turned back toward her destination, running through the servants' door and slamming it shut behind her.

Chapter Eight

MALAYA WAS FEELING BRAVE, READY to face her father and take up the commands that were her birthright.

But when it was Genevieve's father she ended up facing, her bravery faltered. They had run into each other, each going the opposite way through the mountain.

"Where is she?" the Jester demanded. His happy-go-lucky demeanor was gone. He looked very tired, and very angry.

"She went to the castle to find her Frozen Prince," Malaya said, keeping her voice steady, "I'm returning to bring back the royal guard and help her."

"The prince is dead."

"He's not," the Toymaker said, "I saved him."

The Jester sighed, shoulders slumping. "She's up there all alone?"

"No, Roland is with her."

"Oh *good*." The Jester rolled his eyes and pushed past them.

"Be wary, sir knight," the Toymaker warned, "an evil lurks on the mountain."

"I'm not a knight, I'm just a jester," he answered, not looking back.

Candles came to life by magic, lighting the way for Genevieve as she made her way through the castle. She called out, but no one answered. She tried doors, but they were all locked. Torches lining the walls came to life, guiding her to where she was supposed to go.

Not knowing where else to go, Genevieve followed until she spotted something she recognized—a door missing its handle. The prince's room. Now she recognized the hallway, and knew that the Witch's lair was near.

Genevieve jogged forward, ignoring the torches as they turned down another hallway. There! The heavy oak door had sigils carved into its wood, definitely the door of a witch. Genevieve grabbed the handle to pull it open, but a shadowy hand suddenly shot down from the ceiling and placed itself over the door, keeping it shut.

Where do you think you're going?

With a frightened gasp, Genevieve turned and ran back down the hall. She could feel herself being chased— seeing the shadows on the wall darting after her. She felt something grab at her hair and shirt. With a burst of speed, she escaped the clutches and ran into the prince's room. She hit the floor and shimmied under the bed. The shadows followed.

"Come on, please work," she whispered desperately,

crawling deeper under the furniture. She could feel the thing coming after her, grabbing at her clothes and legs. She screamed at its touch and tried to push it away.

The tendrils wrapped themselves around her legs and pulled her out from under the bed. Genevieve cried out as they seized her wrists and waist, binding her as she struggled.

When she was pulled away from the bed she saw a monstrous face staring down at her. It had eyes like storm clouds, horns like tree branches. A long black tongue came out and licked its lips.

Where are you going, little one? Don't you know monsters hide under the bed?

Genevieve tried to retain her composer, but her body was trembling, heart pounding, mind swirling with panic.

"Y-you're the Thing Beneath the Mountain—"

I'm glad I haven't been completely forgotten. But that title doesn't really fit now, does it? Seeing as I'm on top...

Genevieve yelped as the tendrils tightened and lifted her up. Its body morphed and shifted, limbs lengthening as the tendrils retracted back into its body. It released Genevieve and caught her in a long, bony hand.

"Why are you here? Where's the prince?" Genevieve struggled against the hand that gripped her. Its long fingers wrapped around her body, pinning her arms to her sides.

I was taking you to him, before you went off course, the creature said, ducking down and slipping through the doorway. Its body changed again, becoming thinner and longer to fit through the door. It returned to its original shape once in the hall.

When the prince's curse broke, so did my prison. It was his ice that held me captive, freezing me deep inside a cave.

"Why?" Genevieve asked, wiggling in his grip. Her fear was deepening as he carried her down the dark hall into a different wing of the castle.

It's the thanks I get for saving a young boy's life. He wanted to live. He wanted revenge, so I gave him the power to do both, and when I asked for something in return, he fought back.

"Wh-what did you want?" She was trembling again, it was getting cold.

Control.

Torches burst into flame. Genevieve saw blackened stone walls and crumbling structure. The corners were filled with dust and webs and there was a hole in the ceiling where the cold mountain air slipped in.

Genevieve realized they were in the wing of the castle that had burned.

As her eyes adjusted to the low light, she spotted Adrian on the floor, pale and unconscious. She gritted her teeth and struggled with renewed fierceness against the monster, fear retreating.

Wake him for me, won't you?

It squeezed her tightly and she felt claws dig into her sides. Genevieve yelped. It released and squeezed again, harder. This time she screamed.

Adrian jerked and lifted his head, dark hair falling

over his blue eyes. Genevieve saw his chest wound, stitched up but purple and grotesque.

Look who I found... the creature taunted.

Adrian flatted his palms against the stone floor and pushed himself up onto trembling knees.

"He needs a doctor," Genevieve said, gasping for air, "please, let him go."

Certainly. If you agree to stay.

"Don't listen to it, Genevieve," Adrian said gruffly, "it has no power."

I didn't, but now... The thing held Genevieve out, opening and flattening its hand so that she fell across its palm. It used its thumb to roll her onto her back, and press down into her stomach. Genevieve tried to wiggle away, but its fingers formed a cage around her, claws extending and pointing down at her threateningly. It pressed down into her stomach, making her yelp, then ran the pad of its thumb over her breasts. Genevieve cried out in protest, and it caught her shirt in its claw, threatening to tear it away.

"Let her go," Adrian growled, his tone making even Genevieve flinch. He managed to get to his feet and stand up on trembling legs.

Certainly. If you agree to stay.

Adrian clenched his fists. The thing gave Genevieve a little toss, making her scream.

Who is it to be? Who receives the torture, and who gives in? We'll take turns...

Genevieve screamed again as the creature lowered its head to her, opening its mouth to reveal sharp teeth. It wrapped its thumb around her midsection, pinning her wrists down. Its tongue came out and ran over her body, catching her shirt and pulling it up, leaving moisture on her stomach.

"Stop!" Genevieve screamed. Another lick and her shirt came up, the tongue brushing the underside of her breasts.

"Take me," Adrian sighed in defeat, "have it your way. Let her go and take me."

Aw, I was hoping you might hold out a little longer. He stroked his finger across Genevieve's body and gave her another squeeze. *I like how she squeals.*

It dropped Genevieve, unceremoniously letting her hit the ground with a cry of pain. It leapt over her and jumped on Adrian, pinning him to the floor like a predatory feline.

I need your full consent, otherwise this starts all over, and next time I'll start inflicting pain.

Adrian took a deep breath and shut his eyes.

Genevieve stumbled to her feet, ignoring the pain in her body, trying to run toward the creature and knock it off of Adrian. She saw it morphing into shadows and slip into Adrian's eyes and mouth. She cried out and ran forward, arms outstretched to stop it.

She raked her hands through the shadows, falling forward in an attempt to tackle it, but she only fell through and landed on Adrian's chest. The last of the shadow disappeared, slipping inside of him, through his parted lips and half-shut eyes.

All went still.

"Adrian?" Genevieve touched his face. His hand came

up and grabbed her wrist. Adrian opened his eyes, revealing the blackness that had taken over the irises. He smiled at her.

Genevieve yanked herself away and stumbled back, hitting the floor.

Adrian rose up to his feet, testing his hands and feet. "*A physical form at last,*" he said in a voice that was not his own. Shadowy tendrils flowed out from his hands and back, shooting toward Genevieve. She tried to dodge the attack, but they wrapped around her body, holding her in place.

"*And my powers as well. This mountain is mine once again.*" He chuckled darkly, throwing Genevieve down and pulling her toward him. He leaned down on one knee, looking down at her as she was dragged across the floor.

He grabbed her chin and licked his lips. "*You can still be with your Prince Adrian if you wish it. I can feel his desire for you, twisting around inside of me. It's quite delicious.*"

Genevieve struggled, pulling her head out of his grasp. "I will beat you out of him!"

The creature in Adrian's body suddenly frowned. "*Keep struggling,*" he ordered.

Genevieve glared at him, but did try to free herself from the shadows.

His frown turned into a smile. "*I like how you wiggle.*"

Genevieve looked down and realized he was becoming aroused, cock straining against his pants.

"Don't touch me," she hissed through gritted teeth.

"*So, this is what an erection feels like. It's quite... insistent, isn't it?*" He leaned forward, placing his hands on either side of her head and pressing his body against hers. "*Oh yes.*"

"Get off!" Genevieve screamed, thrashing against him.

"*Come now, it's still your Adrian. You can still be with him. Become my queen…*"

"You need a father's consent first." A voice caught them both off guard. The creature looked up, only to be met with a face full of wooden plank. The blow sent him reeling, flying off of Genevieve and onto his back. The tendrils retreated.

The Jester grabbed Genevieve's arm and pulled her up, pushing her behind him.

"Are you alright?"

"Dad, that's not Adrian," Genevieve said, "It's some sort of monster that's taken over his body, you can't kill him."

"I can do plenty of other things," the Jester said, patting the plank against his palm. The creature pushed itself up, blood flowing from its nose.

"*The downfalls of a physical form,*" he grumbled, spitting blood from his mouth.

"I have an idea," Genevieve whispered, "I'm going to the witch's lair to find a cure. Hold him off for me."

"What?" The Jester turned, trying to stop her, but Genevieve was already running out of the room. The Jester turned back to the creature and readied himself.

"*Do you plan on killing your prince, puny jester?*"

"No, but I'll beat the shit out of him." The Jester raised his board and charged forward.

• • •

Genevieve ran through the halls, panting for air as she pushed herself to run as fast as she could. It was a little difficult navigating the blackened hallways, but after a few twists and turns, she found herself back in the room's hall, back to the Witch's door.

She grabbed the handle and pulled it open. It led to a spiral staircase, and she took it in twos, going down into the strange laboratory, where a caldron sat cold over an empty fireplace. The top shelves were lined with books, and Genevieve proceeded to pull them all down, sorting them by titles that might help her.

The Jester cried out as the tendrils grabbed him and threw him against a wall. He slid to the ground and struggled to catch the air that had been knocked out of him.

The creature approached and looked down at his crotch in annoyance. *"I'm still hard. Can a male human find relief with another male?"* he wondered, wrapping the Jester up in his shadowy tendrils and pressing him up against the wall.

"Sorry, sweetheart, you're not my type," the Jester said, struggling against his binds. The monster tilted its head.

"It's true, you're not quite as satisfying as the girl. Where did she go? Are you distracting me so she can escape? Because the woods are filled with my eyes, I'll easily get her back."

"Too bad you're busy with me," the Jester grunted as the tendrils tightened.

The creature grinned. *"Indeed. I'll have to go find her."*

He dropped the Jester and turned away, walking

toward the exit. The Jester stood up and picked up the piece of wood he had dropped during their scrimmage. He pulled it back and threw it with all his might. The wood spun through the air, set to strike the creature in the back of the head.

A shadowy tendril shot out and stopped the assault, grabbing the plank out of the air. The creature looked over its shoulder at the Jester, smiled, and threw the wood back. It struck him squarely in the forehead and sent him crumbling to the ground, unconscious.

Genevieve flipped through the books frantically, searching for anything that might help. The books were poorly organized, and some lacked titles. Some weren't books at all, but journals in the Witch's own hand.

What did she need against this monster? Could she draw a sigil? She didn't know the ingredients for a proper potion. She did find plants used for banishment, but was that the same thing?

With a sigh of frustration, she began searching the jars and boxes. She found some of the dried leaves from the banishment recipe, but one—a soapwort flower—was still missing.

That was when the door opened.

Genevieve looked up in terror as the creature in Adrian's body stepped inside, smiling casually.

"Ah, the Witch's old room. Not a bad idea, but it won't work."

He stepped toward her. Genevieve straightened, her eyes hard. As he reached for her she back flipped away from him, then summersaulted to the side. His eyes narrowed and the tendrils appeared.

Genevieve dodged them, using the acrobatics she learned from her dad to jump, dive, and roll away from his grasp until she was on the other side of the room. She ran through the door and up the spiral stairs, leaves clutched in her hand.

She heard the thing give chase, it's footsteps echoing around her as she ran down the hall, into the main foyer, and out the front door.

She almost crashed into Roland, who stood in the snow, covered in blood and looking haggard. Their eyes widened at the sight of each other, but before words could be exchanged, the monster came running through the door. Roland looked up and pulled a dagger from his belt. His quiver was empty.

"Run, I'll hold him off."

"Don't kill him, I know a way—" Genevieve was cut off from further explanation as the monster came after them. Roland leaped forward, brandishing his weapon. Genevieve kept running. She needed soapwort leaves, and soapwort grew near bodies of water. There had to be a creek around here somewhere.

She heard a cry of pain and surprise behind her, but she couldn't look back. She kept going, running into the trees, trying to pick up the sound of flowing water over her own pounding heart and gasping breath.

Pain seared through her side as her muscles clenched, and the wounds in her back reopened, dripping blood behind her. Genevieve slowed until she collapsed to her knees, close to tears from the pain and the desperation.

She found herself thinking of Hanna.

"I'm not making the same mistake you did," Genevieve whispered, not unkindly, "I'm not going to lose him."

She pushed herself up, crawling, then getting back to her feet.

When she looked up, she saw Death standing there with someone standing at its side. The ghost of a little girl.

Genevieve's mouth dropped open. "M'kala..."

The girl nodded, still silent. She looked up at the Grim Reaper, who nodded to her. She turned back to Genevieve and pointed.

Genevieve looked in the direction the girl indicated and started to walk. She heard the sounds of running water and moved more quickly. She saw the birds watching her from the trees, and recognized the shadowy look in the eyes of a rabbit that jumped from the bushes, but she didn't care.

She broke through the brush, finding a creek on the other side. She began searching the ground, trying to find the soapwort. The plant could survive in cold weather. There had to be one, had to be...

She saw movement in the corner of her eye and looked up. M'kala and Death stood across the water, watching her. M'Kala pointed down at her feet. Genevieve recognized the little soapwort plant growing there.

She walked across the creek, ignoring the icy water as it rose up to her knees. Tears rolled down her face, blood stuck to her shirt. She made it to the other side and stared at M'Kala, who continued to wait, almost apathetically.

"I know your dad," Genevieve gasped.

M'Kala nodded.

"Th-thank you, for showing me." She stared at the Grim Reaper worriedly. "Have you been waiting here for her? Waiting for her to complete her unfinished business so you could take her?"

Neither of the specters answered, but Genevieve felt it must be true. She had heard plenty of ghost stories before, and they all spoke of phantoms struggling to complete an unfinished task before moving on to the afterlife.

How long had M'Kala waited after the Witch had killed her? How long had she haunted the castle to make sure the Toymaker and Adrian were set free?

"I won't let you down." Genevieve sank down to her knees and picked the leaves from the soapwort, crushing them in her hands with the others.

The Grim Reaper touched M'Kala's shoulder, and the two specters disappeared as Genevieve looked up.

Behind her, she heard footsteps, snapping twigs, and crunching leaves. She lowered her head and placed the mixture of plants into her mouth. She heard the splash as someone walked into the water, then she felt a hand grab her hair firmly, pulling her head back.

Adrian glared down at her. "*There's no one left to hold me back now. If you still wish to fight, I will kill you.*"

Genevieve didn't answer, only stared up at him with an empty expression.

"*Good.*" The tendrils returned, wrapping around her

waist and pulling her off her feet so that she was at eye level with the monster. Its dark gaze stared into her. The tendrils squeezed, making her wince. *"This has become quite tiresome."*

It reached forward and pulled her shirt down, cupping her breast in its hand. Genevieve winced and squirmed. The thing smiled. *"That's better."*

He pulled her forward, hands grabbing her body, and lips encasing hers. Genevieve opened her mouth and pushed her tongue forward, along with the mixture of plants, shoving it into his mouth.

The creature balked and tried to pull away, but Genevieve wrapped her arms around his neck and held him to her. She forced her tongue into his mouth, shoving the plants into the back of his throat.

His teeth bit down on her tongue, and Genevieve cried out, pulling away. The monster coughed and choked, and Genevieve kept a grip on his head, digging her nails into his skull.

"Give him back!" she shouted, pressing her lips against his again. He struggled and fell to the ground, body twisting and contorting as if in pain.

She remained on top of him, forcing the kiss on his lips so that he couldn't spit out the concoction. She felt something rushing past her, flying through her hair and brushing over her skin like a strong wind. She kept kissing, eyes shut tight, while its hands beat against her, trying to push her off.

Slowly, the struggles stopped, the wind died away,

and when Genevieve opened her eyes, she saw Adrian's staring back at her.

"Adrian?" she gasped, finally ending the kiss.

Adrian smiled, eyes shimmering with tears. He grabbed her in a tight hug, burying his face in her neck. "Oh, Genevieve..." he gasped.

They both heard a growl and Adrian reacted immediately, rolling them over so that his body shielded her. Genevieve looked over his shoulder and saw the Thing Beneath the Mountain, glaring at them from the shadows of the trees.

It charged, teeth bared.

Adrian raised his hand.

Genevieve turned her head as a flash of cold hit her. She blinked in surprise, finding that she now lay in a fresh pile of snow, the creek was frozen, and the monster was covered in a harsh frost that sealed its eyes.

Adrian looked at his hands in surprise. "I guess a piece of your curse stuck around."

The thing snarled and backed away. Adrian advanced on it, calling up a cold wind to blow around them.

"Go back under the mountain."

With one last growl, the creature turned and ran away, melting into the shadows, and disappearing.

Adrian turned to Genevieve, hands trembling. Genevieve stood up and ran forward, practically falling into him as Adrian wrapped her up in his arms. She sobbed into his chest.

"I was so w-worried. I th-thought I couldn't get you b-back."

"You *did* get me back. My amazing Genevieve," Adrian cupped her cheeks in his hands and lifted her head so he could smile down at her. "You saved me."

They embraced again, snow falling gently around them.

The flurries died down as they stumbled back to the castle. Both weak and hurting. They found the Jester and Roland at the castle gates, not looking much better, but alive.

"Bastard tossed me around like a sack of potatoes," Roland grumbled, rubbing his shoulder.

"Tell me about it," the Jester answered, sporting a large and colorful bruise on his forehead. "You yourself yet?" he demanded as Adrian and Genevieve appeared.

"I am." Adrian nodded.

The Jester smiled at Genevieve. "Glad to see you got him back."

The sound of horse hooves and carriage wheels suddenly filled the air. Everyone looked toward the road.

"It must be Malaya!" Genevieve said.

"Then that's my cue," Roland said quietly, standing up.

"Remember what I told you," Genevieve urged, touching his arm as he passed. He nodded to her, then ran for the trees, just as the carriages pulled up.

Malaya stepped out triumphantly, shouting orders for the knights to secure the castle, and for the doctor to see to her friends. She ran to Genevieve, and flung her arms around her.

"I did it, Gen," she whispered in her ear, "I took

charge. You should have seen me. You should have seen the look on Papa's face!"

Genevieve giggled and hugged her back. "I'm proud of you."

Malaya pulled away and looked up at Adrian instead. "So, this is my would-be kidnapper."

Adrian bowed low. "Hello, your majesty. My apologies for any trouble."

"To the doctor with you, Prince Adrian," Malaya said indifferently, "we'll discuss apologies later."

Adrian nodded, smiled at Genevieve, and allowed the doctor to take him inside for treatment. Malaya helped Genevieve follow them inside, while the knights assisted the Jester.

"Where is Roland?" Malaya whispered.

"He's safe. He didn't want to be caught by the guards. I know you'll see him again."

Malaya sighed, but accepted the news with dignity. "I do hope so."

They stepped inside the castle, and Genevieve's eyes found Adrian. She watched as he removed his shirt so that the doctor could look at his wounds. Adrian met her gaze and smiled.

Genevieve smiled back. Malaya found a couch so she could lay down. Genevieve dozed off. Eventually, someone tended to her back, placing new gauze over her cuts. Someone else gave her something warm to drink. She hardly remembered any of it as she slipped in and out of consciousness. At one point she woke to find Adrian sitting over her, stroking her hair.

"Go back to sleep, my love," he whispered.

She woke to find her father. She tried to tell him that she had seen a ghost, but he only quieted her back into slumber.

Her dreams were filled with snow.

With everyone taken care of, and Genevieve asleep, Malaya excused herself and stepped out of the castle for fresh air. She looked toward the tree line ruefully, part of her wishing she had stayed.

Would she ever see him again? Where would he run to next?

"You know," a voice snuck up on her as the Toymaker approached her. He had stayed by her side the entire time. When Malaya stood up to her parents she looked to the Toymaker, who encouraged her with silent nods. It felt like he was the only one on her side, and it gave her the strength to command her parents and command the royal guard into going up the mountain. "Sometimes a good long walk is all you need to really clear your head."

"How long of a walk?"

"Oh, about a half mile due west, not that far."

Malaya looked at him, and he winked. "There's a mill on the creek, separated from the rest of the village. It's a good place to hide. A nice, private place."

Malaya smiled, and started walking.

She found the mill as the Toymaker had promised, abandoned. Inside, she found Roland, resting on a pile of hay and burlap bags.

When she came in he raised his head, startled, but smiled at the sight of her.

"Malaya…how'd you find me?"

"Well, as royalty, it's my job to track down fearless rogues," she stepped inside and sat next to him on the hay, "and thank them for helping me."

Roland took her hand and kissed it gently. "Anything for you."

Malaya sighed. "What happens now?"

"Whatever you want to happen."

"I know what I *want* to happen," Malaya said, "but it's not what everyone else will allow."

"Oh, I don't know." Roland pulled her down so that she was lying next to him, face to face. "I saw you giving orders when you arrived. I have a feeling not many will dare challenge you now. Besides," he pushed her dress up to rub her thigh, "there's no rush. I'm happy to be with you in any way I can. Even if it's just like this, sneaking into mills for a little while."

Malaya leaned forward and kissed him. She felt Roland smiling around her lips.

"I want that too."

"We'll find a way, princess," Roland said, pulling her closer, "I don't think I could let you go."

"Touch me again, Roland, please."

Roland complied, his hand traveled further up her dress until he could grab her ass. Malaya felt her cheeks blossoming with a blush.

"How far do you want to go?" he asked.

"I want to touch you."

Roland turned to lie on his back. Malaya unbuckled his belt, seeing that he was already erect beneath his pants. She pulled them down, revealing his cock.

Malaya's blush deepened.

Roland stroked her arm, smiling reassuringly. "Take your trousers off."

She did so, slowly pulling the sleeves away and letting the garment fall to her feet. Roland took her in, staring at her naked body. Malaya sat on her knees between his thighs and took his cock in her hand.

Roland released an exquisite sigh at her touch. Malaya began to move her hand up and down, enjoying the blissful look on his face. She messaged his balls in her other hand.

"Faster…" Roland begged.

Malaya complied, tightening her grip and pumping him with vigor. She watched as he wiggled under her touch, sighing and moaning. She felt herself becoming wet at the sight of him. She yearned to be closer.

She leaned forward and placed her lips on the head of his penis. He answered with a sharp intake of air. Malaya gave him an experimental lick, running her tongue from the base of his dick to the slit at the top, taking in the taste of him. There was flesh and sweat, yes, but something more. A sensual smell that made her smile. She wrapped her lips around the top of his member, sucking as she continued to pump.

Roland gasped, a soft "oooh" of surprise slipping out of his mouth. He reached forward and pulled the cock from her lips just as he came, white seed spilling out over his stomach. He released a deep sigh as his body went limp. In a burst of inspiration, Malaya leaned forward and licked his cock, making him shiver.

"You naughty girl."

Malaya giggled. She fetched her handkerchief and cleaned him up, rejoining him in the hay. They encased each other in their arms and kissed deeply, safe in the silence of their sanctuary.

Chapter Nine

THE SNOW HAD FINALLY MELTED ON the Northern Mountain as summer moved into the region. Late blossoms filled the trees and green leaves began to appear.

Genevieve leaned eagerly out the carriage window, admiring the fresh foliage. The Jester had taken her back to Malaya's castle, and Adrian had agreed with him. They both insisted that she needed proper rest and recovery, and Adrian's ancient home was no place to do it.

When they arrived, Malaya's father helped them to track down proof of their royal lineage. He took the news with good cheer, finding the whole thing very funny.

"As you are no longer my jester, what shall I call you?" The king asked.

"I don't know what title suits me now, but my name is Nathaniel."

The king promised to help Nathaniel reclaim the castle as long as they remained allies. Nathaniel happily agreed, and the king promised to send jewels and livestock as soon as they were moved into their new home. Her father no longer wore his jester outfit, he dressed in a linen shirt, cape, and a grand hat with a plum. People called him "Lord Nathaniel" now.

Genevieve received letters from Adrian, who reported back to her about the state of her new home. With the help of Malaya's father, they were able to organize a remodeling of the castle, getting the place cleaned with new furniture moved in. He was also overseeing the redevelopment of farmland and livestock to make the palace profitable again. In his letters, he reminisced about repopulating the village one day.

Genevieve wrote back, saying that she knew just the man who could help, if he didn't mind pardoning a criminal.

Once she was well enough, she insisted on returning to the castle, even though the renovations weren't complete. Malaya offered a carriage as long as she got to come along, and the girls reminded their fathers that they were perfectly capable of running away to the mountain on their own. Nathaniel quickly agreed to take them.

As they neared, Genevieve saw that many laborers were working around the castle. Windows were open, the scorch marks of the past fire were being scrubbed away. Gardeners tilled the land, and the road had been smoothed.

"Wow," Malaya said, "he's been cleaning up."

The carriage came to a stop and the girls stepped out. Nathaniel jumped down from the driver's seat as a stable hand came up to take their horses. He whipped his cape aside proudly, smiling in approval at the sight of the castle.

Malaya was also pleased at the news of Genevieve's royal stature, thankful that they no longer had to hide their friendship. She had made it clear to her father that there would be no marriage until she met a man of her choosing. She agreed to live with Nathaniel and Genevieve for a time to help them throw parties and become acquainted with the other royal families in the area.

"There should be plenty of eligible bachelors that will meet Papa's approval," Malaya said. She was stiff and diplomatic as she said it.

"Maybe some other types of bachelors as well," Genevieve said encouragingly.

Genevieve stepped out of the carriage wearing a beautiful borrowed gown from Malaya. It was the color of lilacs, and hugged her body in a way that she hoped would please the prince.

Home.

She was home.

Genevieve was so focused on reaching the front doors of the castle that she almost missed him, were it not for his amused chuckle that tugged at her ears and turned her head.

There he was.

Prince Adrian stood tall, his pale skin now a healthy pink, his dark hair cut and slicked back. His eyes a warm blue, like a beach-side bay.

Genevieve stared at him, voice lost.

"I've come as a suitor, my lady," he said. A breeze

picked flower pedals off the trees and cast them around his body.

Genevieve leapt toward him, throwing her arms around his neck. She could feel the bandages under his shirt, where his wounds still healed.

"Careful now," the voice of the Toymaker broke up their reunion, "he's still recovering."

Genevieve released Adrian and hugged the Toymaker instead. "I'm glad you're back."

"Me too. I'm officially the butler now, but I'm hoping to be kept busy with new toy orders very soon." He patted her back reassuringly, and bowed his head to the prince. "Remember now, don't strain yourself."

Adrian's eyes hadn't left Genevieve. He stared at her with a relieved, and hungry, smile. "Absolutely not."

The Toymaker rolled his eyes, but left them to their privacy.

Adrian grasped Genevieve's hands. "Come with me."

"Where are we going?"

"I'm stealing you away. Old habits die hard."

Malaya sat alone in the carriage as they drove back down the mountain. Now that Genevieve was safely delivered, she needed to return home to finish packing for her move into Prince Adrian's palace. She stared out the window, daydreaming, when the carriage suddenly came to a halt.

"Bandits have blocked the road m'lady!" she heard the driver call out.

Her heart skipped a beat. "Oh dear."

She heard men shouting, felt the carriage shaking,

then the door opened, and the Bandit of the North looked in at her, grinning widely.

"I'm robbing your carriage, your majesty."

Malaya beamed back at him. "Whatever will I do?"

Roland grabbed her hand and helped her out. The driver was being held, unharmed, by Roland's companions, who winked and gave him a thumbs up.

"I'm afraid I'm taking you hostage, m'lady, but don't worry, we should have you back before dinner." Roland helped her up onto his horse, and mounted up in front of her.

Malaya hugged his chest tightly and kissed the back of his neck. "Ride on, my outlaw."

Roland urged the horse forward and they rode off into the mountain. Malaya pressed her breasts against his back and squeezed his hips until Roland became impatient, brought the horse to a halt, and turned sideways in the saddle so that he could turn his face to her. He grabbed her waist and kissed her deeply.

"How far are we going this time, princess?" he whispered against her lips, slipping his hand up under her dress to squeeze her thigh.

"Far away, my rogue." She gasped as he kissed the tops of her breasts. "To the ends of the earth."

Genevieve giggled as Adrian pulled her away from the castle, touching her shoulders and stroking her hair as he guided her through the trees.

"I can't believe you're alive…"

"Death has always had a loose hold on me." He

pushed her against a tree and kissed her deeply, slipping his tongue between her lips. Genevieve breathed in his smell.

"Why did you break the curse that night?" she asked as he broke away. "Why did you kiss me, knowing that it might kill you?"

"I lost everything when the rebellion came to the castle. I didn't want to lose anyone else. Not you, not the princess, not even the Witch. I was happy to go with Death if it meant everyone else was safe."

"You never did intend to take Malaya, did you?"

He shook his head, staring down at her. His fingers caressed her cheeks.

"You knew what the Witch was up to."

He silently nodded.

"But you took me."

His hands left her cheeks and clutched her shoulders instead. "It was wrong of me," he said quietly, "but when I saw you there...the girl I had watched grow up inside the crystal ball...I couldn't help myself. I saw a chance to thwart the Witch, but more than that, I was in love with you, and I thought..."

He touched his chest where his wound lay.

Genevieve pressed her hand against his. "I'm glad you did."

With a relieved smile he kissed her again, and pushed the straps of her dress away. Genevieve fumbled with his belt, pulling it from his pants.

The prince cast his cloak into the grass and they laid upon it, eagerly exploring each other. Adrian took his time slipping the dress from her body, and when it was off he leaned back to take in her naked form.

"You're so beautiful."

Genevieve felt her face turn red.

He fell upon her, kissing her body. First her collar bone, then the swell of her breasts, then down her stomach...

Genevieve gasped when his tongue touched her clitoris. He put his lips around it and sucked. Genevieve moaned and let her body go limp, as if she were melting away. He teased her there for a while before slipping his tongue into her womanhood. He grabbed her hips and pulled her down around his mouth, licking and pressing.

Genevieve panted with arousal, craving more. She reached down and touched his face, grabbing his hair. Adrian allowed her to pull him back up into her reach. She kissed him, tasting her own flavor on his lips.

She lifted her legs and hooked the top of his pants with her toes, sliding them off. Adrian kicked them away. His cock pulsed with expectancy as his erection grew. He pressed himself against her vagina, wrapping her body in his. Genevieve hugged him in turn, moaning with pleasure as he pushed himself inside her.

"You're so wet," he whispered, taking her ear lobe in his mouth. He eased himself in and out, slowly, agonizingly. Genevieve mewled and tried to speed up his thrusting. The prince chuckled. "No, you don't."

He grabbed her wrists and pinned them above her head. Genevieve felt an icy coldness grow over her arms, and she gasped in surprise. Adrian released her and straightened up, but her wrists would not move. They were frozen to the ground.

"This magic is useful," he said, swirling a fingertip over her breast. The iciness of his touch made her smooth nipples rise and harden, becoming extra sensitive as he pinched them.

Genevieve whimpered for mercy as he played with her, pressing her nipples between his fingers to make her arousal grow, but still only giving her the slightest attention down below.

In and out...in and out...

"A-adrian..." she begged.

"Yes?"

"P-please...oh I want to come..."

"You will, but first...promise you'll marry me." He sent a sharp thrust into her, sending a shock of pleasure through her body.

"Yes..."

"You will?" Now his voice grew tentative, almost surprised.

"Of course I will," Genevieve grinned, happiness swelling up inside of her.

Adrian fell upon her, slipping his tongue into her mouth in a deep kiss while thrusting inside of her with vigor. Genevieve let out a cry of satisfaction around his mouth. He slipped his arms under her back and held her close.

Genevieve screamed out as she orgasmed. She broke her wrists free from the ice and wrapped them around his neck, pressing their bodies tightly together as he came inside of her, gasping from his release.

He remained inside of her, melting against her body as Genevieve stroked his back and kissed his cheek, his ear, his jaw. Adrian only held her tighter.

The sun warmed their naked bodies, and the flower pedals fell like snow.

About Minna Louche

Minna Louche has a Master's degree in English, and uses her talents to create stories that are both passionate and well-written. Follow her on Twitter: https://twitter.com/LoucheMinna

Dear Reader,

Thank you for reading *The Frozen Prince*! Many books thrive or perish based on reviews or a lack thereof. Please consider posting an honest review on the site you purchased this book from and/or on Goodreads. If you're new to writing reviews or wouldn't know how to write one, you could start by sharing what you found most enjoyable about this book.

Also, be sure to sign up for the Deep Desires Press newsletter. This is the best way to stay on top of new releases, meet the authors, and take advantage of coupons and deals. Please visit our website at www.deepdesirespress.com and look for the newsletter sign-up box at the bottom of the page.

Thanks again,
Deep Desires Press

WIN FREE BOOKS!

Our email newsletter is the best way to stay on top of all of our new releases, sales, and fantastic giveaways. All you have to do is visit deepdesirespress.com/newsletter and sign up today!

SUBSCRIBE TO OUR PODCASTS!

Deep Desires Podcast releases monthly episodes where we talk to your favorite authors—or authors who will soon become your favorite!

Deep Desires After Dark features sexy excerpts read by our fabulous authors!

Find both podcasts on Apple Podcasts, Google Podcasts, Stitcher, Listen Notes, and our website (deepdesirespress.com/podcast/). Subscribe today!

Support the Deep Desires Podcast on Patreon and you can receive free ebooks every month! Find out more at patreon.com/deepdesirespodcast!

Don't Miss These Great Titles from Deep Desires Press

The Scullery Maid
Dallas Alexander

Catalina will gladly fight monsters, especially if that means finding her missing father in the dangerous woods around their village. What she's not prepared to fight is a Prince whose lusts are set on her, who will claim her for himself, even if it means taking her captive. Being the Scullery Maid, she has no choice but to submit, but she will never give her heart over to one who is used to taking what he wants, and there's no way Prince Rowland will persuade her. No way at all...

Available now in ebook and paperback!

Raven's Touch
House of Tannin #1
Siryn Sueng & Jessica Collins

Washed upon a foreign shore, Rhys Kelstai finds himself in the company of a very handsome man: Lord Cadeon of Tannin. Having rescued the raven-haired foreigner, Cadeon is drawn to the stranger from a distant land — much like he had been drawn in by a captivating woman some years before. Their thinly veiled desires toward one another slowly deepen, but before either man can act on his wishes, an old threat reveals itself to Rhys. The dragon witch threatens everything that has been building between Rhys and Cadeon, and with the arrival of a past lover even more is at stake.

Available now in ebook and paperback!

Stealing Beauty
Fairy Tales After Dark #1
Jessica Collins

This time, it's the Beast who's going to attempt to tame the Beauty. The only thing he can't protect her from ... is himself.

A modern and sexy re-telling of Beauty and the Beast! Available now in ebook and paperback!

Finders Keepers
Fairy Tales After Dark #2
Jessica Collins

When a sexy-as-sin Dominant shows her a whole new world of whips and restraints, Jayla wants to trust him, but the scars of her abusive past are in the way.

An almost-too-hot re-telling of Aladdin! Available now in ebook and paperback!

To Love This Woman
Patricia Pellicane

Everyone Georgiana ever loved has died. Now three months short of gaining her inheritance, she must spend her last summer at Castle Montgomery with her Aunt Millicent, and her abominable cousin, Jonathan Manning, the Earl of Montgomery.

Available now in ebook and paperback!

CPSIA information can be obtained
at www.ICGtesting.com
Printed in the USA
LVHW091343040619
620100LV00026B/499/P